WED TO THE ALIEN BRUTE

ACCIDENTAL ALIEN BRIDES BOOK 3

JANUARY BELL

Wed To The Alien Brute by January Bell

Published by January Bell

www.januarybellromance.com

Copyright © 2022 January Bell

Cover by Natasha Snow

Edited by Belle Manuel

Interior art by lucielart on instagram

❀ Created with Vellum

AUTHOR'S NOTE

CONTENT WARNING:

Hi readers!

I do my best to write the most fluffy, escapist, fun and romantic science fiction romance possible. The last thing I want to do is ruin someone's day by surprising them with a plot twist that will upset them, so I've included a list of potential triggers on this book.

Please feel free to skip this if you don't want to be spoiled, or use them if you need to!

****

****

**********SPOILERS AHEAD***********

****

****

This book contains references to:
-pregnancy and babies
-violence
-gun violence
-animal death

-post traumatic stress disorder
-religion
-sexually explicit scenes
-torture
-imprisonment
-hostages
-medical tests

BEX

THE OVEN TIMER DINGS, a sound so familiar and homey it almost makes me forget I'm baking inside a hollow tree, like a damn princess. I hustle over to the alien equipment, turning off the clock I scrounged together under the watchful eye of curious Suevans in one of their tech labs. I split my time between there and training and stress baking, it seems.

I open the door, and steam rushes out, leaving me blinking against the heat.

"Fuck yeah," I say, mentally high-fiving myself.

Another batch of faux-cookies. Close enough to the real deal that they help stave off the homesickness threatening to tow the rest of the women under. Well, the six of us left here in the tree house —myza— we all share.

The other two are happily getting their brains banged out by their hot alien husbands. Lucky fucks.

"Those smell so good," a familiar voice says, and I turn to find Gen in the doorway.

"Yesssss," Michelle says, sprinting down the staircase towards the cooling faux-cookies.

"We need a better name for them," I say, putting the baking tray on a soft towel to cool.

"They're cookies."

I scrunch my nose at Gen. "They are not cookies. They're faux-cookies."

"Then call them faux-cookies," Michelle says, practically drooling over the blobs of steaming dough.

"Fuck what they're called, I want to eat them," Gen says, rubbing her growing stomach. I grin at her. She's just so dang cute with her baby belly. She looks adorable.

Not that I'd ever tell her that.

"Fookies," I say suddenly. "Let's call them fookies."

"Uh." Michelle squints at me. "That sounds nasty."

"Sounds like a good time," Gen says, high-fiving me. "Fookies it is."

Oh. Wow. I must be out of it if I didn't even consider the dirty implications of my new pastry nomenclature.

I frown, leaning against the wall and watching the blobs start to contract into disc-shaped fookies. *Fookies.* I snort, but it dies quickly.

"Hey, don't start that again." Michelle sighs.

"I just don't understand why he won't even *try.*" Unlike the other crewmembers, I didn't give a fuck that they married us off to alien warlords. Well, that's not entirely true, because I'm all about choice, and ours was taken away, and I feel terrible for the other girls…

But for me?

It was the moment all my monsterfucker dreams became real.

My accidental alien husband? He checked all my boxes. Hot face, huge muscles, thick hair, green scales, and a *fucking* tail.

Emphasis on fucking.

"She didn't hear a word you just said," Gen's telling Michelle, and I snap out of my horny reverie. "She's probably thinking about his tail again."

"*You* never should have told me about your sex life if you didn't want me to think about my husband's tail!" I hiss.

Michelle gives a long-suffering sigh. "Bex, we've been over this a million times. The rest of the warlords are upset that we aren't overjoyed at ending up married to them. They're keeping their distance from us because we can't communicate, and out of respect."

"I don't want respect!" I yell, grabbing a too-hot fookie and shoving it in my mouth. An action I immediately regret, considering it's roughly the temperature of molten glass. "And what about the Beast and Abby?" I ask through my mouthful, fanning my face. "He was all over her like white on rice the other night."

"The Beast doesn't count," Gen says. "Everyone knows he's the worst of them all."

"Don't fucking talk about me like I'm not in the same goddamned tree house, like we're not all on the same horrible season of *Alien Bachelor in Paradise*," Abby grumps, coming slowly down the stairs.

"We weren't talking about *you*," Gen says.

"We were talking about your husband, though," Michelle says, a slight grin on her face.

"Yeah? Well, he might be crazy, but at least he's crazy hot," Abby says, cracking her neck and eyeing the fookies.

"Was he a good kisser?" I ask her dreamily.

"You're a creep, Bex," Abby says.

I swat her hand away as she reaches for a fookie. "No details, no fookie," I tell her.

"He was fine." She shrugs, but a slight blush colors her cheeks.

"Oooh," Gen says, "Abby liked kissing her husband."

"Shut up," Abby says. "Michelle could tell you more about it than me, Bex. One tipsy night does not a story make."

Gen and I round on Michelle, who blinks owlishly. "I don't know what you're talking about." She sniffs. "Gimme a fookie."

"Is that what you said to Alvez?" I ask innocently.

She scowls at me. "No. We went on a walk. That's it." She gives a half-hearted shrug. "I still can't understand him."

"Ouch," Gen says, her forehead wrinkling.

"What's wrong?" Abby and I ask at once.

She rubs her stomach. "Stupid pregnancy. The baby wants a cookie."

"You can have one," I say graciously.

"What about me?" Abby pouts.

"You can get your fookie from the Beast. The rest of these are for Dergoz." The Brute. My Brute. My *husband*. "And this is the last-ditch effort before I enact my evil plan."

"Oh, God," Gen says through her cookie. "Not that again. Don't do whatever it is you're planning."

I wilt, then return to putting the cookies on a pretty wood platter. "I thought you were supportive of my plan."

"I don't even know your real plan, Bex, considering you won't tell us. I thought Operation: Brute Seduction consisted solely of fookies and sheer discipline. And then maybe a real fookie, if you catch my drift."

Abby snorts, and Michelle lets out a little laugh.

I don't though. My jaw clenches, and my eyebrow does a little twitch.

"Do you even like him?" Michelle asks. "Like, seriously. I know you want to bang him, because… obviously, but you've never even dated anyone for more than a month."

"I like him just fine." I glare at her. "And it doesn't matter because we're already fooking married, and I may as well get the goods!"

Abby winces. "Jesus, Bex, you don't have to yell."

"I am going to bang him, and I am going to get him to pay attention to me," I snarl, feeling unhinged. More than usual, that is.

"Did you mean that in the opposite order?" Gen asks. "Because usually it's the opposite order."

"I don't care," I yell, waving my hand. A fookie goes sliding off the plate, but Abby's there instantly, catching it and putting it in her mouth before I can even react.

"Yum," she says, closing her eyes. At least, I think she said yum, but it's hard to tell with her mouth full.

"I just… I don't think the Suevans think about this the same way we do. The same way you do. And the Brute, especially. He's super serious. Reserved." Gen narrows her eyes at me. "This wouldn't just be fucking for him. You need to be sure you want the whole ball and chain before you lean hard on the seduction thing, my dude."

"Then let's go drop off these fookies and hope like hell it makes him want me," I tell her. "Otherwise we're onto *Operation: Brute Fucking*."

"That sounds painful," Michelle replies.

"Like a yeast infection in the making," Gen says.

"Like you'll need an ice pack afterwards," Abby adds.

"I hate all of you," I say, flouncing toward the door. "Now help a bitch out, and maybe I'll make you fookies later. Gen, you're coming to translate. Abby and Michelle, you're moral support."

"Fuck it, I'm in," Abby says.

"You sure you want us all there?" Michelle asks. Of course, she does, because out of the four of us, she's the only intelligent life form.

"Yeah," I say, and blow out a noisy breath. "Because if he acts like a dick again, I'm gonna need y'all to take me shopping for Operation: Brute…" I pause, unsure of what to call my plan B. Or is it C, at this point? Whatever.

"Brute Love," Michelle says, batting her eyelashes as she holds the door open for me.

"Perfect," I say, despite inwardly cringing.

Love has little to do with what I want from my husband.

CHAPTER
TWO

DERGOZ

A QUICK RAP comes at the door to the myza where I've made my temporary home after the attack at Acriset.

"Fuck," I mutter. My tail lashes behind me, clipping the walls of the tree. I do not wish to be social at this hour. This is my time to unwind. My time to relax and let the day drop away.

I do not have patience for many Suevans, and I certainly do not have patience for anyone right *now*.

I swing the door open, and the female standing at the doorstep to my myza is the absolute last creature I want to see.

My wife.

Two warlords flank her, the humans Gen and Abby, and their intel officer, Michelle, who stares up at me with eyes full of silent reproach. Alvez's wife.

I raise an eyebrow. "To what do I owe the honor? It is not every evening I am faced with a quartet of human females." It comes out as irritated as I feel, and my tail lashes harder.

I can never say the right thing around them. I am not a smooth talker like Kanuz nor an honorable Suevan like Draz.

I will never be able to undo my wife's impression of me.

That I am a *monster*.

Gen translates my words, the only one of the group that can understand anything I say. While she talks to the others, my gaze travels along the luscious curves of the female who wed me. The female who dishonored me by calling me monster.

The female I cannot seem to banish from my thoughts, despite all my intentions to do so.

Her hips flare out more than the muscled women next to her, her thighs thick and soft and begging to be tasted. Heavy breasts sway enticingly under the thin purple fabric she wears, her smooth skin darker brown than the others. Her heart-shaped face is full of good-humor, her brown eyes rich as Mother Sueva's soil.

And her lips… that mouth…

She's talking now, her voice lilting and beautiful. Which made it all the worse when she called me monster. Brute. As though I haven't spent the last few years of my life hearing exactly that.

"I made you some treats, because I thought you might want something to, uh, snack on." A deep red flush colors her cheeks, and I grow hard as I watch her mouth move, the smooth column of her throat bob as she talks. Everything about her is just so damnably soft.

Unlike me. I'm all harsh angles and sharp talons and killer fangs. Made for murder.

"I thought we could talk," she says, a note of hope in her voice that nearly undoes my resolve to send her away.

How much have I wanted this? I have spent my whole life wanting a family. Wanting what was ripped away from me. Wanting a chance at love, at forever, with a female. And now I have one, as beautiful as the sun's beams shining through the asteroid belt, and I cannot stand to be around her.

Because I know what she thinks of me; heard it from her own lush lips.

Monster.

"I have nothing to say to you," I address Gen, who slants her eyes at me, clearly frustrated. I know the human warlord well enough now to see it clearly.

"You should at least talk to her. And if you're not interested, then you should let her go so she can find someone else here. You're acting like an asshole. More so than usual."

Bex's eyes narrow at Gen's words, needing no translation to understand them and draw her own conclusion. Her expression changes from soft and warm, shuttering and becoming cold. Calculating.

I watch her carefully, her knuckles whitening on the platter of treats she's brought with her and her posse of female warlords.

"Is there someone else she is interested in? Someone who is less *monstrous*?" A muscle twitches in my temple, and my tail whumps into a piece of furniture.

"What is he saying?" Bex asks, staring at me intently, as though she can will her translator to work.

"He's acting like a jealous husband," Gen tells her. "He's asking if you're interested in someone else. Someone who isn't monstrous."

"What does that mean?" Abby asks, gaze cutting to the treats and then back at Gen. "They're all monsters. They're scaly fucking aliens with fangs and tails. They're green!"

"Shut up," Gen tells her, and the younger woman presses her lips in a thin line. "They're no more monstrous than humans, or did you forget who sold you out to be here?"

"Was there something else you wanted?" I ask through gritted teeth. "I am not in the mood to entertain company at the moment."

Gen whips her attention back to me, rattling off my question for the rest of the humans.

The corners of Bex's mouth twitch up, her small white teeth showing. She is so fragile, so delicate and harmless in appearance. No wonder they think us monsters.

I hate that they are right about me. *The Brute.*

"I just wanted to see if you would talk to me," Bex says, and there's a refreshing candor in the statement, as well as a resigned expression on her pretty face. For a moment, I want it. I want to talk to her. I want to fix this thing that is broken and painful between us. I crave her flesh like I have craved nothing in my life.

"There is nothing to talk about," I tell her. "Thank you for the…"

"Fookies," Gen supplies, continuing to translate. Their intel officer considers me contemplatively, as though she can read my thoughts.

"Fookie. Thank you for the fookies."

Abby and Gen both crack a smile, and Michelle tips her head back, biting her cheeks hard. Apparently, they all understood their strange human word even when I mangled it. Bex clears her throat, but I hold up a hand.

"I do not wish to speak. I am tired, and I must rest before I leave for Perzivor."

Gen translates again, and Bex simply watches me, hurt written across her face. A strange pain clenches my chest.

"You're leaving for the capital?"

"I have business there," I tell her. "Business that does not involve fookies."

Gen repeats my words. Bex cocks one eyebrow, and behind her eyes, I can tell there is a flurry of activity happening. The rest of her crew are shooting each other repressed grins, and I wonder how badly I have mispronounced the word before deciding I do not care.

All I want is my wife to leave me in peace.

"When do you leave?"

I shrug. "I am scheduled to depart a few hours after nightfall."

"Take your fookies," Bex says, her voice sugary sweet, her lips begging to be tasted. "You never know. You might get hungry on your trip." She shoves the platter at me, and I take it from her instinctively.

I do not have to say another word. I do not even have the chance to.

Bex simply turns on her heel, setting off at a fast clip toward the Market. I should not enjoy how her plump ass jiggles underneath the thin fabric of her pants, but I do.

The rest of the human females stare after her before murmuring their goodbyes and practically chasing after her.

Good. It is good that she left.

It will be easier for both of us if she leaves me alone.

But why can I not bear the thought of her with another?

I slam the door behind me, and a decorative planter falls from the wall, soil and pottery shards exploding across the floor.

Yes. It is better she ran from me, the most monstrous of all Suevans.

BEX

I KNOW *exactly* what I'm going to do.

Nobody, and I mean nobody, turns me down.

Not even my gorgeous, grumpy alien husband. He puts the grump in grumpy. I just need him to *also* put his grumpy in me.

"Bex," Abby calls out. "Slow the fuck down."

I don't, my shorter legs still managing to eat up the ground as I race into the market street. It's never truly busy, thanks to the fact that there just aren't that many Suevans to make it bustle.

But it's busier than the rest of Edrobaz, and I cut through the clusters of Suevan males and the few older Suevan females, like a heat-seeking missile who's locked on a target.

"She has a plan," Michelle says. "Can't you tell?"

"You mean, did we see the deranged light in her eyes? Because I sure as shit did, and I have to say, I'm slightly terrified." Gen sounds like she's right behind me.

"Carpe dickem, ladies," I yell over my shoulder, earning some startled looks from the Suevans.

"That's... that's not the saying, Bex," Michelle says slowly, her eyes round as saucers.

"I don't think she cares," Gen says in a stage whisper, a wicked light in her eyes. Out of all of them, Gen is the most likely to love my evil plan *and* the most likely to stop it from happening.

"Seize the dick," I say even louder, causing Abby to dissolve into laughter. "I don't see the problem."

"That's not even remotely correct," Michelle says, harrumphing as she closes in on me.

It doesn't matter. I've found my target.

"Xez!" I say with all the subtlety of a coked-up fifties housewife. Not that these Suevans would have a clue what that would even mean.

Gen sighs, stepping between us to translate.

"Here she is," the clothing merchant says, a broad grin turning up the corners of his face. "My favorite customer. The most beautiful fruit of all the human females. A flower of femininity. A shining beacon of hope in these dark times."

"Aw, Xez, I bet you say that to all the ladies." I bat my eyelashes.

"No, he doesn't," Abby says, narrowing her eyes at him.

"Warlord Abby," Gen translates, Xez's gaze flitting to Abby briefly before returning to me. "And you have brought the lovely Michelle, and the incomparable Princess Gen. I expect you are here for the many items you ordered. I must say, I have never seen taste as refined as yours. I have never made garments as provocative as these. I have never been so eager to see my creations in the wild."

Gen pauses, turning to me as Xez waits with the air of a wine sommelier waiting for us to return the compliments on his wares.

"What the hell did you buy? And how much?"

I shrug. "Ever heard of a trousseau? Look it up. None of us got married on our terms, but I sure as hell am going to pretend I did. And that means new clothes." The corner of my mouth turns up, and Michelle pinches the bridge of her nose. "And other things."

"That's not even… Trousseaus haven't been a thing in decades.

Centuries even," Michelle says in a pained voice. "Why do I not want to know what's going to come out of your mouth next?"

"I don't know, I'm all in," Abby says.

"Can't say I'm not morbidly curious," Gen adds.

I suck in a dramatic breath, staring at each of them in turn. "You know what they say," I announce.

"Dear God," Michelle sighs.

"Shoot for the moon, and even if you miss, you'll still land on top of the alien cock," I finish.

"That's not…" Michelle shakes her head.

"Live for the nights you'll always remember with the alien dicking down you'll never forget."

"Bex—"

"Shhh, I want her to keep going," Abby says between laughs.

"Yesterday is history," I proclaim, a finger in the air, "tomorrow is a mystery, and today is when you put on lingerie and impale yourself on a massive alien cock."

Michelle scrubs a hand down her face.

"Is that all—" Gen starts.

"Keep calm and fuck an alien. If life gives you an alien, have sex with him. Live every day like it's your last chance to hop on board the alien express." My nose scrunches up as I think hard.

"I think she's out now," Michelle says.

I open my mouth, but Gen claps her hand over it before I can say anything else. "Please. Enough."

Abby just laughs, her hands on her knees, before sucking in a wheezing breath. Michelle stares at me with a pained expression, and Xez's face is frozen in a rictus of a polite smile.

"Anyway," I say, out of cliches to ruin, "yeah. I'm here to pick up my stuff."

Xez hastily produces several packages, his tail twitching furiously behind him. "Here you are. You can pay me any time."

Gen says, her voice shaking with laughter, "Oh no, that's okay, I'm sure I can count out some Suevan coin—"

Xez barks something out, making a shooing motion with his hand.

"He says you're scaring off customers."

"That's rude," I say.

"Is this why you brought us? Because you needed help carrying it?" Abby says suspiciously.

"Do you want to get the fookie or not?!" I yell at her.

"Calm down, for crying out loud," Michelle says.

"You are acting even more unhinged than normal, Chaos Queen," Gen says, shaking her head and picking up a few of the parcels. "What the hell do you even need this much stuff for? Is this part of your plan?"

I grin, feeling a bit like the Grinch as I stare her down. "Oh, Princess, it's allllll part of the plan."

"You know I hate when you call me that," she grumbles.

"What? Why?" I ask her, all innocence.

"Stop trying to distract us all from finding out your plan," Michelle says, tucking one of my boxes under her arm.

I pause for a beat, letting the sounds and smells of the marketplace wash over me, taking in the massive trees cradling the blue Suevan sky.

"The plan is to pack all these pretty new things away, race to the hangar, then take it with me to Perzivor."

"Perzivor? What, like you're going to follow Dergoz there?" Abby asks, also holding one of my purchases.

"No," I say, stacking the rest of the boxes and heaving them into my arms. "I'm going to stowaway on his ship."

My news is greeted by stunned silence. Speechless is about what I expected from them. Not like it matters, because I'm closed to well-meaning advice at the moment.

Nope, Chaos Queen Bex is full throttle ahead only, no rear views, no second thoughts, no analysis. I'm done with that.

The time for action is here.

DERGOZ

I AM ABNORMALLY restless after Bex saunters away. The walls of the myza seem to close in on me, and I pace around the main floor, trying to sort my scattered thoughts.

No matter how I try, the infuriating female refuses to be banished from my mind. The lines of her body carving an indelible mark, the erotic pout of her lips stained in my memory.

I take the platter of treats she's made for me and slide the lot of them in the trash.

"Hmph," I grunt.

My comm tablet chimes, and only too happy for the distraction, I pick it up immediately.

"Warlord Dergoz," Draz says, his face filling the screen. His scar stands out in stark relief to the green scales on his face, a mark of his prowess at surviving.

"First Warlord," I greet him.

"There's been a slight shift in priorities based on information Nydo the Roth shared."

All thoughts of my wife blessedly vanish from my head. "Yes?"

"Can you be ready to leave earlier? We have a different flight plan we must discuss, as well."

Anticipation tingles through me, all my senses coming alive at the thought of a mission. At finally being able to strike against the Roth.

"I will be there immediately," I tell him.

"If there is anyone you wish to say goodbye to," Draz grates out, his eyes serious, "I would do so."

I blink slowly, knowing exactly who he means. A snarl curls my lip.

"That will not be necessary, Draz." I disable the comm before he can reply and will myself to believe my own statement.

If Draz thinks I need to say goodbye to Bex, it means he's sending me into a potentially volatile and dangerous situation.

"Fuck," I grit out, my talons scraping against the hard back of the tablet. My tail slams into the floor.

I find Bex's comm link and leave her a voice message.

"I will be leaving sooner than I anticipated. Thank you for the treats." I cut my eyes to where they sit in the garbage. "That was *kind* of you. If I do not return from my travels, I give you leave to seek out another's bed. You can be free of your monster husband once and for all."

I close out the tablet, leaving it behind.

If Draz plans to send me into enemy territory, then setting Bex free of me is the least I can do.

Even if the thought causes my hands to fist at my sides.

———

"Dergoz," Draz greets me, helping Alvez and the new human warlord Juls haul equipment into the hybrid spacecraft. Part long-distance hauler, part planetside jumper, the ship's perfect for missions that require the ability to adjust on the fly. The strange appearance helps it blend in, too, not sleek enough to be tagged as

Suevan right away, too junky to be thought of as more than another settlement craft.

Except it's not, not at all. It's rigged with weaponry, advanced stealth tech, and a warp core that makes traveling long distances a breeze.

"That serious, eh?" I ask, eyeing the ship.

"The Roth managed to remember that Nyria V49, the small moon orbiting Mearus 9, holds the location of a secret operations base," Draz says.

"And all it took was mentioning the registration numbers and specs of his brother's ship," the female Juls adds brightly. Alvez lets out a throaty chuckle of appreciation.

Juls is one of the few females able to actually understand us, something that's made her valuable to keep around in addition to her skills and intelligence. As long as her warlord husband stays on mission, she's a focused asset to the team. I fear that as soon as he returns to Edrobaz to seek her out, her focus will… shift. Her husband would certainly like it to.

Unlike Abby, who is as surly as the Beast she's married to, Juls is pleasant to be around.

"How long are you planning to hold Nydo's brothers in orbit?"

"They are safe," Draz answers. "And we treat them well. They were happily watching Suevan vids, the last I heard. But they are too valuable a lever to send on their way when we have a Roth officer in our cells."

"So the mission," I say, shoving a heavy crate into the cargo bay of the ship. "Is it reconnaissance? Just a fly by, send a drone in, see what comes out?"

"Not exactly," Alvez says slowly.

Juls' eyes narrow. "Nydo says that they store information there. A databank."

"You meant to tell me that Nydo, the Roth whose *brothers we are currently holding hostage* in orbit, has offered up a Roth data storage facility?" I shake my head. "It sounds too good to be true. Surely, you see that. I am very likely walking into a trap."

"That is why we are sending you, Brute," Draz says, a note of finality in his voice. "You are the best equipped to go in quiet, and rain chaos and fire on them— should it be a trap."

Adrenaline sings through my body, my tail flicking wildly behind me at his words.

Because he is right. I am the best candidate for this mission.

"You will conduct the reconnaissance mission, and you will retrieve any and all information you feel is vital in our war against the Roth. Suevan settlements are priority—"

"As are their plans for Earth," interrupts Juls. She ignores the pointed look Draz shoots her.

"Oh, good, you're here." Draz's wife glides into the hangar, carrying another crate.

Draz takes it from her, and she smiles up at him in such a loving way that my throat tightens in envy. What would it be like to be lavished with such an emotion? I shake my head. It is the least of my concerns, at the moment.

"Did they brief you already?" Ni-Kee asks, brushing her hands together.

"I did, my heart," Draz tells her.

Juls rolls her eyes, and Alvez does his best impression of an invisible Suevan. Unlike the Beast—he lacks the genetic markers for that—he simply manages to loom with an awkward expression.

"I wish you would have waited for me. Did you tell him about the convoy?" Niki asks.

"The First Warlord did not," I tell her.

"Then I'm glad I showed up when I did. There is a Roth convoy en route to Mearus 9, possibly Nyria V49. We don't think they will be there until after you are safely off planet and spaceside, but we also know the Roth love their little surprises."

I stand stock still, calculating the danger. An unknown facility reconnaissance mission, a Roth military convoy expected to show up, apparently, shortly after the First Warlords want me spaceside.

It is not ideal.

It will be dangerous.

And it might be the thing to protect the human females from being hurt by another monstrous alien.

"Are you still game?" Ni-Kee says, her expression flat, devoid of all humor. This is the warlord, not the warm human Draz calls his heart. "This could be the mission that turns the tide against the Roth."

"I do not understand what game you reference," I tell her, "but I am willing to go. I am willing to do what must be done to protect our people—and yours."

"Good," Draz says, clapping me on the back. "Then come with me, and let us go over the finer details of the facility. Nydo was generous enough to draw us his best rendering of the schematics of the databank, as well as how many potential Roth units are deployed there."

I start to follow Draz and Ni-Kee from the hangar, and for a moment, something catches my attention at the hangar gate, but when I look again, it's gone. I squint into the dark recess for a moment, but nothing moves.

"Come," Alvez says. "You do not have time to stare at shadows and brood, my friend."

"I was not brooding," I snarl.

"Are you feeling all right, then? A Brute who is not brooding…" He trails off, grinning at me.

I bare my fangs at him, and he lets out a small chuckle before following me from the hangar.

Still, I cannot rid myself of the feeling that something watches me.

BEX

MY HEART'S hammering in my chest. Literally, it feels like it's going to jump right the fuck out and do a little dance on the weird-ass spacecraft in front of me.

I thought he fucking saw me. For a split-second, I was sure Dergoz *had* seen me.

There had been a shit ton of warlords here, too, all talking in low, serious voices. The kind of voices that always meant bad shit was going to go down. I spent long enough in the Federation after the Roth invasion to pick that up.

Which left me… unsettled.

And now, wedged in between a crate twice my size and the cool metal wall of the futuristic Suevan space hangar.

Maybe this is a terrible idea.

A stream of guttural consonants pour out from beside me, and I nearly jump out of my skin.

"What the fuck?" I yell, nearly dropping the weird duffel/box combination thing I'd packed all my favorite outfits in.

The Suevan guard's eyes grow wide, and I glare at him as he continues to jabber at me in a language I wonder if I'll ever understand. The worst part is, I'm one of the best techs on Earth, and I can't make heads or tails of why our freakish symbiont translators keep failing.

The Suevan steps closer, his diamond-pupil eyes narrowing as he tells me something urgently. Oh. Shit. Okay, I need to deal with this, or I'm going to end up in the cells I know span underneath this building, thanks to Abby's loose lips.

"You think I'm not supposed to be here, I know, but that's only because—" I straighten, fixing my expression in my best impression of my mother's stern glare. "That's only because you weren't told about it. I am joining my husband on this mission. Captain Jacks, the First Warlord's wife, and my superior officer, told me to be here."

I don't add that she told me to be here, like… at this building, in general, tomorrow, so we could have lunch. But technically, it's not a lie.

Misleading, sure. Untruthful, yeah.

A lie? Eh.

The Suevan's eyes narrow even more.

Right.

"My husband is going on this ship, correct?" I say, snapping the words out like a drill sergeant. The Suevan responds immediately to that tone, standing up slightly taller. Compared to me, he's much, much, *much* taller, but I am not about to be intimidated. Much.

The Suevan soldier responds, and by the confused slant to his features, I'm assuming it's an affirmative.

"Then I am supposed to be here."

The guard points at me, then the ship, then the doors at the end of the hangar.

"I know he's not here, and do you know I can't understand you? It's very rude to talk at someone like that." Actually, I don't care at all, but I do need him to let me on the damn ship.

When he takes me by the arm, about three different ways I could play it rush through my frenzied brain.

1. I could go limp and pretend to faint, thus securing a diversion that I would… not be able to get out of, because *I* would be the diversion.
2. I could fight—and lose. I don't have a weapon, and the Suevan is about three times my size.
3. I could keep bluffing and see what happens.

Door number three it is. Bluffing and gambling go hand-in-hand, and despite Michelle's words about Dergoz resonating through my head in a very uncomfortable way, I decide that's the hand to play.

"There's a reason they call him the Brute, isn't there?" I say, doing my best sneer at the guard. It's damn hard to look down your nose at someone who's at least three feet taller than you, but I'm doing my best!

The guard's eyes widen a little, and he tugs me again, farther out from the crate and the wall.

Fuck.

If anyone else sees me now, the gig is up.

I have to get on that fucking ship.

"You don't want to find out why they call him the Brute, do you? You don't want to know firsthand, do you?" I keep my voice low. Dangerous, like I heard Gen sound once. I ignore the fact my impression of her just makes me sound like a Barbie doll.

The guard turns a paler shade of green.

Jack-fucking-pot.

Now it's time to hammer that pressure point until he gives.

"If he sees you touching his wife, what do you think he'll do to you?" I ask, ignoring the squirming sensation whispering Dergoz wouldn't give a fuck if he saw the guard hauling me over his shoulder and running off with me.

The guard turns yellow, and I blink up at him as he loosens his hands, holding them both away from me.

"Dzxifb-sjlk," he says.

Right. I squint at him, and he gestures to the ship.

Oh. Oh, shit.

My plan fucking worked.

I push down the urge to sprint for the ship, instead strolling over to it with a flip of my hair, my luggage firmly in hand, like I own the damn place.

Nobody but me knows that my tits are sweating bullets, and no one is going to find out!

Once I'm on the ship, I take a few minutes to situate myself, frowning at the huge cargo crates that appear to be full of everything from advanced tech that I've only glimpsed at the lab I work from, to weaponry so deadly it makes my throat dry.

All this for a trip to the capital?

Maybe he's taking supplies to another warlord there.

Maybe I should worry more about why that guard was so terrified by the mere idea of my husband.

Maybe I should have stopped to figure out why the fuck they call him the Brute, after all.

I open a few of the doors, manually overriding the ship's system with a flick of my fingers on the control pad. Thank goodness I've spent the last few weeks up to my eyeballs in Suevan tech, otherwise I'd really be up a shit creek without a paddle.

The ship's relatively small, with a ton of cargo space, a tiny exercise space attached to a sleek kitchenette, the bridge, and one bedroom. I cackle to myself. Not me, living out my romance heroine dreams of only one bed!

I let myself into the soon-to-be tropetastic bedroom, tossing my case on the mattress, and pulling out the teensy strappy number I had Xez sew up for me.

Well, I may not know why they call him the Brute, but I'm about to find out exactly how he reacts to his wife in sexy lingerie.

By the time I strip down and figure out how to get the damn thing on, though, I'm tired. Probably from the adrenaline overdrive of being found out and bluffing my way onto the ship, or from the fact it's past my grandma-style early bedtime.

I shove the luggage into a closet sized compartment stocked

with state-of-the-art camouflage clothes. My fingers skim over the material, and it shimmers as it reacts to the touch, the fibers mimicking the dusky tone of my skin.

Why the fuck does he have all these in here?

No sooner does the thought cross my mind than the sound of approaching footsteps turns my blood cold. My heart speeds up.

"What if he finds me?" I half-screech, half-whisper.

I slap my arms over the wisps of fabric covering my breasts, then come to my senses as I remember that's exactly the point of me sneaking onto his damn ship.

So he finds me, fucks me, and then regrets ever snubbing me.

Vaulting onto the bed, I arrange myself in the sexiest position I can think of. *Ooh. This bed is way comfier than the beds in the ship we got here in.*

I flop around for a minute, blinking slowly as the familiar thrum of a deep space engine whums into life. Ah, I missed that sound.

Puts me… right… to…

My eyes feel impossibly heavy, my jaw cracking as I yawn.

Sleep.

CHAPTER
SIX

DERGOZ

I SHOULD HAVE SENT my wife more than the one comm message. It was mean-spirited, too. Petty. Regret already tears at me. What if this is the op I do not come back from? What if I die knowing that I never truly gave her a chance?

The ship's controls are familiar under my fingers, the craft neatly entering the atmosphere, clearing the space between the rocks and ice circling Sueva without any problems.

I flick my hands over the screens and panels, putting the ship into warp drive, the stars streaking by the command window. The ship barely strains, barely even feels like it's moving, as it moves beyond the speed of light, into neutral territory, to where the Roth base is located on Nyria V49.

Maybe it's better I told Bex to move on and find another mate if I do not return from this mission. I do not like the thought of her in limbo without me. I do not like the thought of her crying.

I despise the thought of her with someone else.

I grit my teeth, unstrapping the safety webbing and standing abruptly.

Perhaps, when I return to Sueva, I can start over with her.

Perhaps the others are right, and I have been too impatient and closed off around her. Perhaps I should simply tell her how she hurt me.

If I return at all.

I stretch, checking the stats and data the engine computer spits out on one of the monitors. Roughly half an hour until I enter neutral space.

My mind races, continuously landing on the tempting visage of Bex before I push it away, trying to concentrate on the task ahead, on the danger, on refining a plan that will see me leave Nyria whole.

But my body is tired, and I need sleep.

The door to the bridge slides open easily, and I pad through the ship to the sleeping quarters.

I frown at the red image on the lock screen, which says that the room is occupied. Probably a false signal, thrown up because of some kind of coding error. I make a mental note to check it as soon as the ship leaves warp.

I tap in the code to enter the sleep quarters, and the doors slide open with a hiss. I take two steps in before I fully comprehend why the screen registered the chamber as occupied.

It *is* occupied.

There is a female asleep on the bed. And not just any female.

A female wearing the barest scraps of fabric, luscious breasts moving enticingly as she breathes, her eyes shut in sleep. Her face is lax, smoothed out and innocent.

My gaze rakes over her exposed body, and my cock immediately grows hard as I take in the surfeit of beautiful flesh before me.

My wife is asleep in my bed, and I have never been so aroused and tempted in my entire life.

I turn on my heel, pivoting away from what will only lead to suffering for both of us, and stride back to the pilot's chair I vacated only minutes prior.

It isn't until I'm staring at the stars ripping by in the viewscreen that the gravity of the situation hits me.

Ree-becca is on my ship.

Bex, my wife, is going into a dangerous mission with me.

And I cannot turn back with her because our warp drive will need at least two days to cool before we can use it again.

I lean my head back in the chair and try to calm my racing breath.

My tail lashes behind me.

My wife snuck on board. The same wife who has been the most beautiful, torturous plague on me since the first night we met. And now she sleeps sweetly in my bed, wearing the most tantalizing piece of clothing I have ever seen in my life.

I let out a growl, raking a hand through my hair in distress.

What am I supposed to do with that?

What am I supposed to do with *her*?

At first, I thought she was a gift from the many-faced goddess herself. Sheer perfection, long dark hair and tawny skin so smooth I wanted to trace my fingertips all over her, revel in her. Quick to smile, the expression transforming her face from sultry to irresistible.

Starstruck, I could only stare at her as she wed me in our Suevan ceremony, which quickly went to hell, just like our sham of a marriage. They might call me the Brute, and I know I deserve it, but even I would never have tricked a female into mating with me.

The memory alone sickens me.

Still, Bex was not put off by it; instead, she stared at me as though she, too, had won a prize. I thought myself the luckiest of all the warlords, especially as the women figured out what had happened and became increasingly distressed.

Until I overheard her gleefully telling the other women that she would finally have a chance to fuck a monster.

And I realized exactly what I was to her.

Not a husband. Not a mate, or even a friend.

A novelty.

A *monster*.

Something I told myself I would never be again.

I stand at once, my tail slipping through the slot on the chair. Distress stings through me, and I narrowly avoid smashing my tail into the control panel as I pace the small bridge.

Fuck.

Now she's here, a tempting morsel wrapped in scraps of silken fabric, her skin begging to be caressed, when I know she only wants to seduce me because of some strange proclivity she feels towards monstrous males.

My stomach churns.

Whereas I want a partner.

I want a mate. I want someone to come home to at night and hold in the smallest, darkest hours, when memories crowd so tight and claustrophobic that I wake with my heart in my throat.

I want someone to wake up to, to watch sleep in the morning sunlight, someone I can treasure and care for. Someone who cares about the male I am, not just what I have done in the past... or what I look like.

A snarl rips from my throat.

And now the tiny human who I thought might be that is here. In danger.

I cannot decide if I am angrier at her or myself as I walk the length of the bridge yet again.

Because maybe, just maybe, if I were a better male, if I had not made certain choices during the Settlement wars, I would not be a Brute.

I would not be just a monstrous amusement to my *wife*.

CHAPTER
SEVEN

Bex

Ah, fuck, I fell asleep.

I stretch, trying to get my bearings as I blink wearily, figuring out what woke me up. Not the mechanic hum of the engine, which I love. Not the bed, which is way bigger than anything the Federation gave us, and *way* more comfortable. Another plus in the Suevan category.

Not the temperature, which is perfectly comfortable. I frown, staring at the double doors. Did Dergoz come in? Was it the sound the doors made?

Because it *was* a sound, I realize. A sound woke me up.

The ship jerks, and my eyes go wide, my mouth dropping open as horror starts spiraling through me. The sound that woke me up was the ship leaving warp.

We're not headed to the fucking capital.

We're somewhere in deep space.

Shiiiiit.

This is… not ideal. Fuck. I bolt upright, my mind clicking at way too slow a pace, still sluggish from my accidental nap.

This is terrible. I need to find out where we are headed. I need to find out if there's enough food for me. I need to get my shit together, and fast. This is not the romantic week away I thought it was going to be.

And it's all my fault. Fuck.

I bury my head in my hands, trying to collect my thoughts, trying to figure out how I'm going to survive whatever is in store for us.

Okay. I blow out a breath. My hands steady, the slight shaking subsiding.

I can do this. I am a damn good tech, one of the fucking best. I am Rebecca Abbas, Chaos Queen, and I can do anything I set my mind to. I love being in space. I love the challenges.

I am a goddamn asset.

And maybe, just maybe, this is the perfect way to show Dergoz how valuable I am, how lovable I can be. My nose scrunches. Not that I want him to love me; I'd settle for sex.

I don't need anyone to love me.

I love myself enough for everyone.

Breath gusts out of me slowly as I try to relax. No sooner have I stood up, then the doors hiss open.

Dergoz stands there, his chest heaving, his diamond-pupil eyes wild. Gah, he's so damn handsome and otherworldly. My heart does a little flip.

Swoon.

His gaze heats, traveling over me in a way that makes every inch of my body stand up and pay attention. I swallow hard, and his attention cuts to my throat, then my mouth, and finally back up to my eyes.

"Put some clothes on," he snarls.

I jut out a hip, immediately irritated. "Is there something wrong with what I'm wearing?"

He steps closer, his eyes flashing, tail swishing behind him so hard it slams into the doorway. "You are not wearing clothing. You are wearing a *promise.*"

I can't resist a little shimmy, just to prove the point. His eyes immediately home in on the movement.

Ha. Gotcha.

My breath catches. "Is that a bad thing? Maybe I want to make good on it."

His expression is furious now, though, but I can't seem to stop pushing.

"Why won't you talk to me? Why won't you even look at me?" It comes out whinier than I'd like, and I blink against the sudden sting of tears. "You married me, and now you treat me like dog shit you stepped in on the street."

He blinks so slowly I see his third eyelid retract, which, I admit, is weird. But cool, too.

"I treat you like that? You, who called me monster in front of all your friends? You, who treat me as some sideshow amusement you would like to fuck?"

My eyes go wide as I realize Michelle was right. He's furious with me. I hurt him.

I *hurt* him.

"Oh." I can't think fast enough to explain his accusation away.

"Oh," he mimics, and for a moment, something like sadness flashes across his face.

"I didn't... I didn't mean it like that. I don't think you're a monster." I scrub a hand across my face. How the hell am I supposed to explain my monster romance book love affair with a husband who thinks he's the monster?

Oh, man, I fucked this up between us. Shame burns through me.

Wait. *Wait.* It dawns on me then, what's suddenly so different.

"We're talking," I say excitedly, gesturing between us. "You and me. I can understand you. Oh, this is great. This is great!"

I squeal, leaping onto his chest and hugging him hard before I realize that's likely the last thing he wants. He's stiff, and I start to slide off him, embarrassment heating my cheeks.

Until his arms wrap around me, holding me tight enough that his claws prick against my skin.

"Now is not the time for this," he says, his voice deeper, huskier, than normal. "I am glad you can understand me now, though," he adds, and it's contemplative.

"That might be the nicest thing you've ever said to me," I tell him, disentangling myself from him and patting him awkwardly on his big ole biceps. "See, I don't think you're a monster."

"You do, and I am. It is what everyone thinks. And now you will see what I am capable of firsthand, because you made the idiotic choice to sneak on board."

"I didn't know you weren't going to the capital," I tell him. "I wouldn't have stowed away if I knew you were on a mission. But I can help," I add quickly. "I'm a great tech. I'm a Federation soldier. Where are we?"

"We are headed some place so dangerous—" Dergoz steps so close my breath catches "—so dangerous that they told me to make peace with you, because there was a large enough chance that I would not return to do so."

"Fuck me," I breathe.

"Absolutely not," Dergoz snarls.

"I didn't mean it like that," I say, but a shiver of excitement tingles through me all the same. "Unless you want to."

Focus, Bex.

"It's an expression," I continue, ignoring his scowl. "Kind of like what you overheard me say. It's not a command. Not right now, anyway."

He growls low, and I can't help but arch an eyebrow at him.

"You are not worried about the danger?"

I lift my chin up, my hands on my hips and my take-no-shit expression firmly in place as I take in all nearly seven feet of him. "I am a highly trained Federation soldier. I survived the Roth invasion. I've been coddled on your planet like an infant for the past three and half weeks instead of being able to do basically *anything* helpful. I didn't want to be a warlord because responsibility is not my bag, but I also don't want to just laze around and eat bon-bons all day."

"What is a bon-bon?"

"It doesn't matter," I huff. "Regardless of what either of us planned for this trip—this little excursion—I'm here now, and I am good at my job. I can help."

"You are a fragile, fickle human female," he says. "You are my wife. I will not endanger you. You will stay on the ship."

Ooooh, no he *didn't*.

"Oh, *now* I'm your wife?" I ask sweetly, batting my eyelashes. "Is that right? Now that you want something from me, I'm your wife. But when I want something, you ignore me for weeks on end." I step closer, the rage fires burning so brightly I'm sure smoke's coiling out of my ears. I put my hand on his chest, pushing him away. Or, at least, I try to. I frown as he doesn't budge. Stupid alien muscles.

"No. I'm here now, and you're my husband as much as I'm your wife, which means I can help you and I will. So fuck right off!" I'm nearly yelling by now, so irritated and frustrated that I've nearly lost my head completely.

"Is that what you want me to do? To fuck off, with you right here, wearing that?" He bends down, so close now his breath gusts across my forehead. "Do you want me to paint my release all over your body, wife?"

"Argh! Normally, I would say yes, but now I'm pissed at you!" I stomp my foot and cross my arms over my chest. "And that's not even what I meant!"

He lets out a small huff of a laugh, and I realize he's teasing me.

I didn't know he had it in him.

We stare at each other for a long moment, both clearly bullheaded enough not to budge.

The ship goes dark, red emergency lights flickering on as the overheads wink out.

"Breach detected," the ship's computer chimes. "Losing power."

He stares at me for a beat before whirling around and storming through the bedroom door. I follow, hot on his heels, er, tail, a silky ribbon floating behind me.

"I can help," I tell him, my pulse spiking and my bare feet slapping along the cold metal floor. Maybe I should have put on something over my lingerie, but it's not like clothes are necessary for fixing whatever the hell's wrong with the ship.

"Do you even know how to work Suevan tech?" he retorts, casting me a dark look over one shoulder.

"Just because you haven't spoken to me in weeks doesn't mean I've been sitting on my ass pining for you." *Much.* "I've been working in the tech labs, learning as much as I can. Which is a lot. Also, you're an ass. Take the help and the L, buddy."

"Then give me the L, if you want me to take it." Dergoz's words are confused, his tail flicking close enough it nearly slaps my knee.

"Never mind," I sigh. "Just point me in the direction of the ship's computer."

"Docking sequence initiated," the computer says.

Dergoz turns slowly, and we lock eyes.

"Shit," I breathe.

"This is not a computer problem," he says, running a hand through his hair. It sticks out around his forehead, giving him an adorable, rumpled appearance.

"Docking sequence has begun," the computer says.

"How would you know? This is the first you've understood me, and we've already had a fight."

"And now we're being boarded by either pirates or worse," I add cheerfully.

He gives me a disgruntled head shake, then points to the bedroom. "Go hide."

"No," I say. "I know there's a shit ton of weapons here. Give me a gun."

"I am your warlord," he says, a muscle twitching under the soft scales at his temple. "You will follow my orders."

"Nah, you're my husband, and I'm going to do what I fucking want." I grin, turning to pry a lid off a crate. I wrinkle my nose as I take in the contents.

Not weapons.

"Fruit?"

"It is our cover," he says. "So if it's pirates, they can take the fruit and go. Or, worse, they will take you and the fruit. So I suggest you hide." He heads into the bridge, tapping some of the advanced screens and staring at the results.

"I am *not* hiding," I grit out, firmly annoyed. Maybe it was better when we couldn't understand each other.

"It is not pirates," he finally says, resigned. "It is the Roth. A small ship. Maybe two, three foot soldiers tops. A scout."

"Oh, *fuck*," I say, pinching the bridge of my nose.

This just went from bad to worst-case-scenario.

"The good news is, they won't give a shit about your fruit," I tell him, plucking out one of my new faves and chomping into it. Juice drips down my chin, and I swipe it away with the back of my hand.

"They will give more than one shit about you, though," he growls.

"Likely," I say, and then an idea dawns. A bad idea. Or maybe it's a good one. Really depends on how it works out.

"I do not like this look on your face," Dergoz says testily.

"Well, you're going to dislike what's about to come out of my mouth even more," I say sweetly.

He makes a guttural noise of pure disgust, and I snort, but manage to choke on my own spit, forgetting how to breathe for a second, and start coughing.

Dergoz crosses the distance between us in seconds, patting my back and then opening my mouth, looking for a foreign object, presumably.

"What the fuck," I say, swatting his hands away. "Don't put your hands in my mouth unless we're doing the nasty."

"I do not know what *the nasty* is, but I assure you I do not want to do it with you."

I glance down at where his cock bulges against his trousers, and then raise an eyebrow and give it a significant look. "I wish you weren't a liar."

"Incoming passengers," the computer says.

"You have shit security protocols," I tell him.

"Is your plan to insult me?"

"No," I say, second guessing my hare-brained scheme already. "My plan is to distract the hell out of them while you sneak up behind them and, uh, do whatever it is you do that scares everyone to death."

He snarls at me, showing a whole hell of a lot of fang.

"That's so sexy," I tell him, adrenaline turning me into an absolute weirdo. "Super into it."

"You were wrong. I do not just dislike it. I despise what you just said. You will not show yourself to the Roth. We already know they need females as badly as the Suevans do, thanks to the virus. Besides, I do not need your help."

"That's the beauty of it, Dergoz," I hiss, irritated and scared and full of volatile nervous energy. "That's why I'm a distraction. They're expecting your scary, scaly ass. They're not expecting tits and legs." I stick my leg out, striking as sexy a pose as I can.

He blinks at me.

The docking door hisses open, and his diamond pupils expand as he realizes we're out of time. He hits the floor, and I climb to the top of the crate, feeling exposed and, frankly, completely insane.

Well, I've always been on team use what you've got, and right now? Right now I've got *all* my assets on display.

My bare feet slip, but I pull myself up to the top, grateful for all the free time I've spent hitting the Suevan training ground.

A liquid-sounding voice says something, and my translator

fires at me immediately. Thank fuck that little symbiont bitch decided to finally start working.

"Put your hands in the air," the Roth says, the visor of his field suit rising up as he stares at me. "It's a human female," he says slowly, and the second Roth enters the cargo bay, staring at me with round, dark eyes. They look a lot like humans, except they're as big as the Suevans. Velvety grey skin, swirls of darker shades that ripple across their muscled bodies. All that's covered up by these soldiers' suits, but I've seen enough in close combat to know what they've got under there. Fast healing, super strength, and fucking psychopathic tendencies.

No tails, though, which is *truly* a mark against them.

That and the fact they murdered tons of humans when they invaded Earth.

"Sure thing," I say breathlessly, refusing to look toward the faint noises Dergoz makes as he crawls across the cargo bay and through the crates.

The two Roth scouts raise their energy rifles, aiming them at my chest.

"No talking," says the lead Roth.

"I like her voice," the second says, a strange orange fire burning through his pupils.

Cold sweat slicks my palms. This was the worst idea I've ever had. Too late to think like that, though!

"What about singing?" I say, using the most sultry voice possible, trying to adopt a sexy pose while simultaneously managing not to slide off the top of the slick crate.

"Why are you on the cargo crate?"

"Where are your clothes? Why isn't she dressed? Is this how human females dress?" The last two questions seem to be addressed to the other Roth, so I simply bat my eyelashes and try to figure out what the hell I'm doing on top of the crate in lingerie.

This was… a bad plan.

The sound of metal-on-metal grates across the cargo bay, and the two gray aliens swivel immediately, pointing their guns at where I'm sure Dergoz has retrieved some sort of weapon.

Time for my own big guns.

I thrust a hip out, throwing one hand up in the air dramatically. The effect is somewhat ruined by the fact both my hands are already in the air, but what else am I supposed to do?

"Mary had a little lamb," I croon, doing my very best sexy karaoke to the first song that popped in my head.

The Roths' attention pivots back to me, and I glide one hand over my arm suggestively.

"Mary had a little laaaaaamb," I repeat, shaking my boobs at them.

Out of all the fucking songs to sing sexily at gunpoint to a pair of killer aliens, I had to pick *Mary Had a Little Lamb*? I am seriously fucked in the head.

Their attention is, however, fully focused on me.

"What is it doing?" One asks the other, who shakes his head in sheer befuddlement.

"Maryyyyyy had a little lamb, who's fleece was white as snow." I half turn, spanking my own ass as an impromptu percussion instrument. The slap heard round the galaxy.

"What is a lamb?" one asks, agog as I undulate from my dangerous position on top of the crate.

Dergoz appears behind them, an energy sword primed in his hand. I sing louder, knowing that weapon makes a telltale whine.

"AND EVERYWHERE THAT MARY WENT, THE LAMB WAS SURE TO GOOOOOO!" I scream-sing. *Eat your heart out, Ariana Grande.*

Dergoz stares at me open-mouthed, something like shock and awe washing over his face.

"Now is your chance," I keep going, widening my eyes meaningfully at Dergoz. "You should get two little lambs, whose fleeces are grey as... snow," I add lamely, doing my best twerk, which is to say not good at all. The sheer athleticism and grace it takes to twerk is one thing, and doing it on top of an alien cargo crate in deep space is another.

However, it does seem to be good enough to keep the two horny Roths distracted.

Dergoz gives his head a slight shake, then he *moves*.

The Roths go down hard, each with an explosion of air from their lips.

I stare at him for a moment, shocked. His expression is blank. Haunted. Flat. They didn't even have time to react. They didn't even know he was there.

He *didn't* need a distraction, that much is for damn sure.

The two Roths are limp on the floor. "Are they… dead?"

"No." The word snaps out of him, rife with an emotion I can't place. "They are not dead. As much as you asked for the Brute, I will not do that unless it is necessary. This was not a necessary time."

I decide I don't want to know what he thinks will constitute a necessary occasion. A shiver wracks me, involuntary, all the stress simultaneously leaving my body. My foot slips. I start to slide off the crate, my balance completely off—literally *and* figuratively.

My brain registers this too late, and the next thing I know, I'm clawing at air.

But Dergoz is there, the energy sword clattering to the floor as his hands sweep out, catching me from mid-air.

His bare chest is warm, and it helps settle me. I squeeze my eyes shut, taking a deep, shuddering breath.

"I have you, Bex," he says. "You are safe now. You are with me."

When I open my eyes, he's walking me away from the Roth, stepping over them gracefully, and I have to look away again.

I know what the Roth do. I was there when they invaded Earth.

But it's been a long time since I've had to walk over a limp body, and I always hoped I would never have to do it again.

Always knew that when the Roth are involved, it would be a possibility.

"What are you going to do with them?" I ask, my voice small. "If they don't report in—"

"I will put them on their ship and make it look like their engine malfunctioned. They won't be able to report anything. We can take their comms down. They will simply float in space for a week or two. It should give us enough time to get in and out of Nyria."

"Okay, but if you do it wrong, it will trigger a code with whomever they report back to. You know that, right?" My voice is still shaky, and I swallow hard, ashamed of the fact that the sudden violence bothers me so much. If I were tough, like Niki or Gen, I would have been the one to do it. I would have leapt in there like a badass. But I'm *not* tough like that.

I grip Dergoz's neck even harder, trying to stop the involuntary trembling in my arms.

He blinks down at me.

"You didn't know," I say. "Okay, I can do it."

"You are not *touching* them," he snarls.

"Ew, as if." I stare up at him in irritation. "I don't feel like hauling around Roth at the moment. I was volunteering to help you plant the code that will make the ship malfunction in a permanent manner. It'll look totally natural. You are more than welcome to be the one lugging their unconscious bodies around, my friend."

"I am not your friend," Dergoz says quietly, and for a second, my heart hurts at the intensity of his words. "I am your husband. Now put on something else, because I cannot stand to look at you in this… contraption one moment longer."

He places me on the bed, so gently that my mind has trouble reconciling it with the extreme violence I just saw him deal to the Roths.

And then he's gone, the doors shutting behind him, leaving me alone in his sleeping quarters and with my scattered thoughts.

DERGOZ

I HATE THIS. I hate that my wife, my one chance at happiness, is here. I hate that she risked life and limb to climb up on a cargo crate and dance and caterwaul like a troblek in heat to distract them. As though I needed the help. Sighing, I trudge towards where the Roth lie unconscious in the cargo bay.

I cannot say I did not love the way she looked doing it.

Her spirit simultaneously drives me crazy and draws me to her, and either way, it keeps me constantly on my toes. She is brave and intelligent, unexpected and unlike anyone I have ever met.

I need to figure out how we are going to make this work.

Both on this mission… and *maybe* as husband and wife.

The emergency lights cast strange shadows on the ship, gleaming off the slick surface of the cargo crates. I do not want Ree-Becca taking unnecessary risks. I do not want her clambering to the top of a storage crate and wriggling seductively in front of other men, clad in nothing but the barest slip of fabric. I do not want her thinking I need her to do that.

I do not want her in danger.

My fangs bite into my lower lip, my molars grinding together. Perhaps I have been selfish, holding my hurt deep inside where it could fester. Perhaps it was… childish of me.

I should have tried to talk to her before.

All that time on Sueva, wasted, and now we may not get that time back.

I have been a *fool*.

The Roth are still out cold, their breathing deep and even. I grunt as I haul one over my shoulder, the lights bathing their uniforms in deep red. Unceremoniously, I grab the remaining scout's ankle and drag him toward the docking door. His head bangs against a lip in the floor. I activate the door, untroubled by the welt surely developing on his skull even now.

"I feel like I should feel bad about the fact you're dragging him around like a toddler with their doll, but… it's kind of cathartic." Bex's voice startles me, and I look back at her reflexively.

She's changed, wearing tight fitting armor the human females seem to prefer for training. I swallow, unable to tear my gaze away. This might be worse than the sorry excuse for clothing she wore before. Her hair tumbles over one shoulder, as unfettered as the female's very spirit. Every perfect curve of her body is outlined, the snug uniform accentuating the bounty of her flesh. A possessive snarl grows in my throat.

I want to bury myself in her.

The Roth on my shoulder stirs, and I rap him sharply on the head, still transfixed by Bex.

She winces. "He's going to feel like shit when he wakes up."

"They're fast healers."

"That's gonna leave a mark," she says, but she's grinning at me, as though the thought pleases her. Shame fills me, as it always does, when I think on how the human's planet was left unprotected. We should have helped them. We should have stopped the Roth from ever getting that far.

But we did not.

Sighing heavily, I turn back to the door, smacking the Roth's head on the wall as I turn too quickly.

"Here," Bex says, sliding between the panel and my hand, tapping away on the screen like she's the captain of this ship, like she owns the whole damned place.

The confidence of this small, soft female steals my breath.

Sure enough, the docking gate slides open, revealing the enclosed gangway suspended in space and leading to the scout's ship. Bex nimbly picks her way through the tunnel, clearly unaffected by the miniscule corridor or the vast press of space all around us.

Surprise sifts through me at her nonchalance.

It's something that took me years to become inured to, hardened over decades at war with the Roth, decades spent shuttling from settlement to settlement, defending our people, and creating fodder for memories that will haunt me until my dying day. And still, despite all my time in its cold embrace, being spaceside still chills me.

Bex squints at me over her shoulder. "What's wrong?"

"Nothing is wrong. Why would you think something is wrong? Everything is fine," I say hastily.

"Riiiiight," she says. "Suit yourself. But instead of standing there with two unconscious Roth, maybe you could pick it up a little? You know, hurry?"

Had I been standing still? I suppose she is right. Miffed, I drag and carry the Roth to the end of the docking tunnel, where Bex easily overrides the Roth system, allowing us entry onto their vessel.

"You are talented," I tell her, strange pride filling me at her prowess.

"Oh," she says, her cheeks darkening slightly. "It's not talent, it's just a lot of hard work."

"It is both, my—" I pause, my mouth nearly forming the words my brain cannot reconcile with her yet. Like my body knows what my head will not allow it to say.

"Maybe it is." One shoulder shrugs. "Either way, I worked my ass off to learn how to do this."

"That is not true," I tell her, allowing my gaze to dip to her decidedly present, absolutely artwork of an ass. "Your supple seat is quite visible in those pants."

A startled laugh comes out of her, and she glances sidelong at me before winking. "Had no idea you were an ass man. That is, uh, good to know."

"An ass man?"

"You know, like, you like butts? You're into the butt?" She shakes her bottom, and a low growl rips out of me.

"I am into *your* butt," I tell her. The Roth behind me lets out a pained groan, and I turn, kicking him squarely in the jaw.

The door to the Roth ship hisses open, and a gust of heated air rushes through the tunnel. Bex pays it no mind, even though it lifts her hair on a breeze, making her even more alluring, sending her intoxicating scent all around me.

I could drown in it.

"My perky posterior?" Another wriggle. "My cute caboose? My heavenly heinie? My bodacious badonkadonk?" With each strange word, she thrusts her hips, forcing my mind to obscene places.

My throat goes dry. "I do not know those words." I shake my head. "My translator does not give me a definition."

"Then it sounds like I have a lot about body language to teach you," she says, her voice sultry and alluring and altogether irresistible.

With that, she saunters onto the Roth ship, leaving me staring behind her, at a loss for words and entirely nonplussed at how she's managed to completely upend my entire mission.

Not to mention my ordered, predictable life.

Sighing heavily, I follow her into the searing heat of the Roth ship, the interior darker than Suevans usually keep our ships. It takes my eyes a moment to adjust, and when I do, I immediately drop the Roth dragging behind me, pulling the other off my shoulder and breaking into a sprint.

I pass by Bex, who's blinking into the dark so slowly I immediately realize she cannot see the problem yet.

The problem that's aiming an energy plas rifle right at her.

A third Roth scout.

I do not have time to think through a plan of action, simply continue barreling down the small craft's hallway towards the Roth.

His eyes widen as he realizes I'm not stopping, the barrel of his plasma rifle swinging to aim at me, instead.

The Roth squeezes the trigger, but not before I throw his fellow scout at him, knocking him to the ground with the force of the unconscious body. The Roths make a sick thud as they hit each other, then the ground. Behind me, Bex makes a soft sound of surprise. The pulse from his plasma rifle goes wide, glancing off a ceiling panel, melting through some wiring.

I barely glance at the damage before diving to the ground on top of him, ready to use any force necessary to keep him from getting any ideas about my wife.

BEX

NO SOONER ARE we through the docking door of the Roth ship than complete chaos erupts. Chaos in the form of a mad as a hornet Suevan, using a Roth as an unwitting and unwieldy bowling ball. At first, It's all I can see in the dim light, until the telltale glow of a plas pulse hits the ceiling, the sizzling impact sparking emergency lights to life.

My jaw drops as I discover the reason why Dergoz freaked.

There's a third fucking Roth.

The thrown Roth groans, the sound laced with pain. My nose crinkles as a weird wave of sympathy goes through me. I shouldn't feel sorry for him. His people attacked mine.

But I do, because it must be pretty humiliating and painful to be bodily thrown into someone else.

I don't have time to linger on that thought, though, because Dergoz leaps into action, moving so quickly I can hardly see him in the dark neon-lit interior of the Roth ship. A cracking noise sounds, and the Roth with the rifle makes a guttural grunt before falling limp, too.

Dergoz stands slowly, his tail flicking back and forth in apparent irritation.

"They will not be unconscious for long. Do what it is you need to do." His voice is tight, restrained, like his control and patience will snap at any moment. Tension crackles through his body, and I swallow hard.

"Are you okay?"

"I am fine."

"If it bothers you so much to do this, then why don't you tell them no? The other warlords." No sooner does the question leave my lips than I realize it's the wrong thing to say. Of course, it's too late.

"Because it is my duty, human female. It is my honor and privilege to serve as a Warlord of Sueva." His tone is tired. Resigned. "Besides, the problem is not that I do not like it. The problem is that I like it too much."

I shrug. "Okay, whatever. Suit yourself. I need the main computer access frame."

Dergoz waves a hand to the bridge of the Roth ship, his entire body telegraphing barely restrained violence. His lip's pulled back in a snarl, and I blink up at him for a moment in surprise, hardly recognizing the change that's come over him.

"Are you well, Ree-becca? Unharmed?" he asks as I stare.

"Oh." I haven't ever heard him use my full name. It's… disarming. "I'm fine. Not hurt, if that's what you mean." I don't know what to do with this Suevan warlord, who asks if I am okay. Who catches me when I slip and treats me like spun glass.

Maybe the other women are right.

Maybe seducing him wouldn't be like seducing a rando back on Earth.

Maybe I'm playing way out of my league with this male.

"Are you planning on disabling the ship, or am I going to have to take more drastic measures?"

I swallow, then nod, following as Dergoz storms through the

door to the bridge, his clawed hands ahead of him, like he expects another Roth to jump out at any second.

I don't want to see him eviscerate someone. I've seen enough footage of what the Suevans are capable of; we all have, as part of our briefing before we made it planetside. Spine-ripping and organ-rehoming has never been on my list of must-watch TV, I have to say.

A relieved exhalation surges from me. The bridge is clear. I duck into the captain's chair immediately, my fingers flying over the alien control panel. Disabling Roth ships is one of the first things I learned how to do as a tech for the Federation. It was a key part of our training, a way to take out the enemy as quickly as possible. Take out their exit strategy, pin them in place... and boom.

Big booms.

A cold sweat breaks out on my forehead as memories bubble to the top of my mind.

"My Ree-becca, are you sure you are unharmed?"

"Just trying to focus," I say between gritted teeth.

"You have strange bumps all over your skin. You appear to be expelling water. You have turned a strange shade of gray, and you are breathing heavily despite only the barest exertion."

"You're not helping." My fingers tap a sequence, and the screen blinks black. Fuck. No go. I try another, vaguely aware of Dergoz walking behind me, checking on the unconscious Roth. It blinks black again.

I settle back into the plush command chair, inhaling deeply. Trying to settle myself. Trying to get the sequence right, find the pattern in my mind before I risk a third try—and locking us out again.

"Come on, Bex," I mutter to myself, stretching my fingers and starting over. If I fuck this one up, I could bring hell and fire down on us. I exhale slowly, somewhat comforted by Dergoz's silent presence at my side.

My fingertips tap out a new sequence, and I nearly sob in relief as the computer blinks black—then bright blue.

"I'm in," I tell him. And then I'm flying, the sequences blurring together out of a combination of muscle memory and recognition of the new pattern updates the Roth have installed on these ships. The emergency light flickers. The life support exhales, stuttering before coming back online. The screen flashes different colors as I mess with the systems. I'm like a master pianist, the Roth ship my instrument, as I tell it exactly what I want it to report back to the Roth Overlord and the rest of the fleet.

Engine troubles. Comms troubles. Nothing serious. Report in after repairs in one week. Comms going offline to conserve power. Then I take the comms out, so the Roth scouts can't just ping their Overlord's motherships as soon as they come to.

All reported in a careful arrangement of numbers and symbols, memorized after years and years of study.

Finally, I sit back, exhausted. Drained.

"That was remarkably fast." There's grudging admiration and respect in his voice, and it rankles.

"You didn't think I could do it."

"Not in three minutes flat, no. I do not know anyone that could have done that."

"I thought that's why they picked me for this mission, the original one to Sueva," I tell him. "Because I was the best. Top of my class." I shrug, too tired to do more. "I was wrong."

"No." Dergoz shakes his head, his gaze intent on me. His third eyelid retracts as he slowly blink, his tail still behind him. "You are the best I have ever seen. You are not wrong about that. It is your Earth Federation's loss and my gain. Sueva's gain," he adds quickly, then pushes a lock of wayward hair that's slipped from my ponytail behind my ear.

I suck in a breath at the touch.

"Come. Let's get back to the ship and get on with our mission."

I tilt my head, unable to stand his seriousness. "Oh, it's *our* mission now?"

"You are here. You are capable. It is our mission now," he agrees, helping me out of the chair and leading me through the ship, over the unconscious grey bodies of the Roth.

Our mission. I meant it as a joke, a little tease, but he's so serious.

I like it.

I like that he calls it *ours*, and that he doesn't dismiss me.

My heart squeezes with sudden affection. That, more than anything, scares the hell out of me. All this time, I've wanted to see what Dergoz has to offer, wanted to see what sleeping with him would be like.

I never truly considered catching feelings for the big alien.

I never thought he'd give the chance to.

DERGOZ

REE-BECCA, my Bex, is more than I bargained for. I feel doubly the idiot for pushing her away all these weeks.

Now she's quiet, at my side, as I disengage the Roth docking mechanism. We watch in silence as the Roth ship floats away, the docking tunnel retracting into the base of the sleek scout ship.

"What's next?" she asks, none of her usual lightness and playfulness present. All business. Focused. Her dark eyes are intelligent and raw, and something deep in me responds to it.

This female is like a brilliant gem I once saw at the market, cut so finely that every angle you turned it, a different prism and color of light shone. The closer I look at my female, my wife, the more I learn about her.

And I find that I might like every single facet.

"We get planetside as quickly as possible," I tell her. "We get in, we get the package, and we get out. Alive. Safely."

She nods. "Can do."

"Come," I tell her. "Let's eat and get some sleep. I will put on autopilot and have the ship take the fastest course to the Nyrian surface."

"And there's no interplanetary defense?"

"Not according to Nydo."

"The Roth informant? The one who said there wouldn't be any Roth ships in this sector?"

"You think he lied?"

"I don't trust the Roth, I don't think any of us humans do. But there was a Roth ship out here, in neutral territory."

"One scout does not mean a flotilla awaits."

"Are you defending the Roth?"

"No, I am defending our intel on this mission. I do not think Nydo was aware they would be here."

She pauses, clearly mulling over my words. "Fair enough. I'm not an intel specialist, so I'll have to take you at your word. I just… I don't know. I have a bad feeling."

"Then you most definitely need food and sleep," I grumble. "We will make your bad feelings go away."

She doesn't argue, or make a joke, just assesses me in a silent, contemplative way that surprises me. "Okay."

I do not know how to take this version of Ree-becca. This is not the teasing, sunshine female I've grown used to over the past few weeks. This is a new side of her.

I frown, concern settling like over spiced norlamiz in my stomach. "Tell me more about this bad feeling."

She blinks up at me, surprise clear in the delicate arch of her eyebrows, the crease in her forehead.

Without thinking, I reach to her, using my thumb to smooth the lines away. "I do not like these," I say gruffly.

She huffs a laugh, but it's a humorless sound. "What, my eyebrows? Not much I can do about that, and I gave up trying to change my appearance for a man, er, male, a long time ago. So the eyebrows stay."

"No," I tell her honestly. "I like your eyebrows. They are very expressive. I mean, this look of worry you have. It troubles me to see you… unhappy."

A slow, soft smile curves her lips, her cheeks rounding as she grins up at me. "That was almost nice."

"Tell me what it is you are worried about," I say, the need to soothe her overwhelming, shocking in its strength.

"I just… Something feels off. Why would there be a Roth scout out here, in neutral territory?"

"We are close to a secret base on Nyria," I remind her, unsure of why this bothers her so. It makes perfect sense to me. Of course they keep a few ships in orbit to report back.

"Okay, but it's hardly going to stay a secret if they have Roth ships circling it. That's like waving a red flag." She holds a small hand up, waving it back and forth. "Here we are! Secret base!"

A frisson of fear jolts through me. "It could be a coincidence," I say, but no sooner have the words left my mouth than I know it isn't.

"We're taught not to believe in coincidences. I may not be in intel like Michelle, but I do know that much. Especially where an enemy like the Roth are concerned." She shakes her head, her brow creasing even more. Gently, I stroke the pad of my thumb over the skin there, her cheek resting against the palm of my hand.

"Then let us get planetside as quickly as we can," I murmur. "Let us finish this before anything else can happen." I do not like the fear in her eyes, the same fear that I can feel settling through me, prickly and cold.

A proximity alarm goes off.

Bex's eyes grow wide, then narrow, and we both sprint for the bridge.

"Oh, *shit.*"

My time with the other human females has taught me this is not a declaration of need, but rather an exclamation they use when something has gone wrong.

And as a Roth warship clears the warp ahead of us, materializing in seconds, I can think of no better expression.

"Shit, indeed," I agree. "Strap in."

"Fuck," she says, already pulling the safety webbing over her chest, her skin pale. "Fuck."

"Not right now," I tell her. "But you should know I have not completely decided against it. You are very persuasive."

"What? No. That's not what I— wait, really?" She shakes her head, her long tail of black hair bobbing. "Get us out of here before they decide they want to open fire."

Tail slashing the air behind me, I perch on the captain's chair, strapping myself in before slamming the ship into overdrive, sending it sailing through space and toward Nyria as fast as it will go.

"You're entering the atmosphere too fast," Bex shouts. "Fuck, I hate this part."

Fire burns across the view screens as the ship tears through the atmosphere. The ship's built to withstand all of it, though, and only shakes momentarily as we slip through. Blue bursts around us, so bright Bex throws up a hand to shield her eyes from it.

The computer chirps a warning, and I silence it, not wishing to further distress the small female next to me.

Besides, we already know all too well that the Roth are behind us.

"You're landing too fast, Dergoz," Bex says, her eyes wide as she watches the instrument panel light up. "We're going to crash."

I grit my teeth, eyeing the same panel. "That is why we are strapped in."

"If you crash, how the hell are we going to get off planet when we finish the mission?"

"It might be better if the Roth think we died entering the atmosphere," I say. "Do not worry, though, we will be perfectly safe."

"No. I refuse. You are not going to crash a perfectly good ship on an alien moon. That is not going to happen. We can blow it up after we land safely, I swear to God, Dergoz, do not crash us." Her chest heaves, her eyes wild. Her knuckles are white where she grips the sides of her seat. "Let's at least get clear and get supplies first. Don't crash us, I can't stand it."

"I can do it safely," I grouse, but in truth, I'm concerned about the panic edging her voice.

"Dergoz, please, please," she says, her eyes even bigger.

"If you wish," I tell her, yanking up on the steering. The ship levels out immediately, and she sags against her webbing, her eyes closing briefly. "I would not purposefully endanger you."

"Listen, Dergoz, if you don't like me, you don't have to try to scare me to death to prove a point. Or try to kill me in a crash landing. You can just tell me. I'll leave you alone when we get through this forever if that's what you want. We can get a divorce or whatever it is that Suevans do. There's no need for drastic measures."

I blink at her, the threat of the Roth momentarily forgotten in the face of her panicked words. "You truly believe that is what I wish? To scare you? To hurt you?"

"I'm not Suevan!" she barks, her clear terror giving way to anger. "I can't survive the same shit you can! You crash the ship, I might not make it, Mr. Scales and Tails!"

"Dergoz is fine," I say, confused at the strange name. "You truly think I would do that?" Pain blossoms through my chest, a tight ache that has me sucking in a razor-sharp lungful of breath.

"Dergoz," Bex says slowly, enunciating the syllables carefully. "You've treated me like trash for weeks. I don't know *what* to think about you at this point. But I do know that if you're a lost cause… if *we're* a lost cause, then you can just talk to me and tell me no. I won't bother you again if you really aren't interested." She slants her gaze up to me, fierce and vulnerable all at once.

"I am interested," I say. "I am also afraid that I am the monster you say I am. I am sorry I have hurt you. I am sorry that you think so poorly of me."

And suddenly, just like that, I want her to think the best of me. I want her to see who I truly am. I want her to see beyond my monstrous past and the deeds that have kept my people safe and choose me. Not just for sex, which she's made clear she still wants, but forever.

For marriage and mating.

The webbing snaps off of me with a click, and Bex gives a small squeak of surprise as I close the distance between us in two small steps.

I kneel before her, holding her chin between my thumb and forefingers.

Her throat bobs, her breath quickening.

"I have done wrong by you, my little wife. But I will prove to you that I am no brute, that I am no monster, and that I do not wish you anything but safety and happiness." The words stick in my throat, thick with emotion.

It has been a long time since I have kissed a female, and I stare at her mouth for a long beat, contemplating what it will be like to taste her berry-ripe lips. She might only want me for the novelty, but perhaps that is because I have not shown her who I truly am.

I brush my lips against hers, and she lets out a soft sigh of surprise.

It unleashes something in me, and I swipe my tongue against her lush mouth. She opens her lips, and I growl in approval, need and desire and hope warring within. She tastes better than I could have ever imagined. Sweet as a solman berry, and everything about her is so fucking soft. I groan as she threads her hands around my neck, pulling me closer, deepening the kiss.

Fire snakes through me, a burning need to take this female and show her I meant every word. My free hand fumbles with her safety webbing, and it clicks loose as I gather her small frame into my arms, her strong legs wrapping around my waist, everything about this human female willing and supple and strong all at once.

And so *fucking* perfect.

Her blunt teeth nibble my lip, and I snarl into her mouth, pressing my hand into her ample bottom. She moans again, breaking off the kiss.

At first, I fear I've done something wrong, hurt her, upset her, until I watch the way her lips curl in pleasure, her eyes half-lidded as she tips her head back and grinds against me.

Against my hard cock.

Fuck. I could come just from this. Just from holding her against me, from seeing the pleasure she finds for herself against my body.

Snarling, I capture her mouth again, the need to take her overwhelming and intense. I want to taste every inch of her. I want to show her pleasure. I want to play her body like a perzo drum and hear the music she makes as she comes around me.

Her pretty brown eyes dilate, her cheeks flushed. "We should... We should prepare to land and get clear."

Disappointment wracks me.

Both in myself, for not having the strength of will to give that order.

And in this moment, because right now?

Right now, I do not give a fuck if the Roth find us, as long as I am between this female's legs, rutting her hard and fast.

BEX

OH MY *GOOOOOD*.

I had hoped he would be a good kisser. I mean, of course, I hoped he would be a good kisser. Nobody wants an alien fated mate who kisses like a tentacle monster. Well, maybe that's not true.

But he's a great kisser.

Everything about him is so different from any other man I've ever been with.

His tongue isn't smooth, but covered in small bumps. As soon as I felt them, my mind went straight to the gutter. I want that tongue on my clit. I want him to lick it until I scream.

I'm so wet I can hardly think straight.

And then there was the way he looked at me.

The way he knelt in front of me, held my face, and vowed to make me happy, to protect me.

It was a good thing the safety webbing held me upright, otherwise I might have just swooned straight away.

But now—now he's all business again, back to being Surly McSurlyson, barely speaking to me. I've strapped back into the co-pilot's seat, even though it fits my human body strangely, considering the slot where a Suevan tail would go leaves my butt hanging out in empty space.

I squirm against it, trying to alleviate the building pressure between my legs.

I shouldn't, though, because now all I can think about is how good it felt to have them wrapped around Dergoz. How huge his cock was when I rubbed up against it like a cat in heat.

How he looked at me with something besides callous disregard. How that look set me on fire.

Dergoz is dangerous. Literally and figuratively.

The Suevan is quite obviously a brutal killer, and where that should bother me, it does the opposite. I fucking love it. I feel like he actually can and will protect me, for once, and despite being a very happy independent woman, having a spine-ripping Suevan at my side when faced with a horde of angry Roth is pretty satisfying.

And that scares me. The idea that maybe, just fucking maybe, I like the idea of more than sex with him. Don't get me wrong, the idea of sex with him is still at the forefront of both my mind and pussy, but…

I'm starting to like the idea of Dergoz as… more than a fuck buddy.

A heavy sigh rips from me.

I like Dergoz. He's grumpy as hell, and quite likely my complete opposite… but maybe that's not a bad thing. Maybe that's a complementary thing.

Maybe that's what's been lacking in all the other guys I've dated.

Well, that and scales and fun body parts and that killer Suevan Warlord training.

You know, minor differences.

I just… I didn't expect to catch *any* feelings for the scaly grump.

It's been a long time since I cared about anyone but the crew.

And that's easy, because it's my job. It's been a long time since I had a man besides a fuck buddy.

The weirdest part about this—*we're already married.*

I blow out a breath. My commitment-phobe ass truly got well and bit this time. Can't get much more seriously committed than marriage.

And now it seems like my heart wants to follow suit.

One thing at a time, Bex.

We need to get clear of the fake crash. We need to retrieve the information Earth and Sueva need. We need to get back to Sueva, somehow. Probably on a jury-rigged Roth ship.

Then we can figure out feelings.

I don't have time for feelings. *I never have.*

"You are very quiet, all of a sudden," Dergoz says in a low voice, the ship skating just above the golden-brown grassland. Grass stalks bend as we zoom over them. Something large ripples across the sea of vegetation before disappearing from view again. I squint out the window, uneasy. Anything that big that moves *that* easily is a threat in my book.

"I should have asked your permission before kissing you." He says it so quietly, and it's so far-removed from my own thoughts that it takes me a minute to register it.

"What? Why?" I jerk my head away from the view of the planet's terrain to stare at him. "It was a great kiss. A really good kiss."

"You are very quiet now. I thought perhaps I—"

"No," I tell him, shaking my head. As mixed up as I feel about… well, *marriage*—I don't feel mixed up when it comes to wanting him. "I have wanted you to kiss me for weeks. And I can't believe you're even saying that. It's not like I've been subtle about wanting a magical dicking down from you."

"Magical?" He frowns, course-correcting before glancing over at me. "I do not have a magical cock. I only have a xof, same as every other male."

I raise my eyebrows. Now we're getting somewhere. "A xof? You know, the other women wouldn't tell me what that is." And it pissed me the fuck off, because from the way Niki and Gen whispered about it, it sounded like a fun time. Assholes.

"Perhaps I should not either."

I harrumph, and then he surprises me, shocks me, even, by grinning at me.

The smile transforms the harsh angles of his handsome face, softening it, making my heart melt a little. *Oof.*

Then the ship rattles, the landing gear making contact with the deep grass, knocking me physically off-balance, matching my emotions.

A blinking screen catches my attention, my translator slowly spitting out a readout for the strange Suevan language.

"It looks like a Roth ship is entering the atmosphere," I say, pointing at the screen.

I might have wanted a distraction from my tangled-up feelings, but that is most definitely not the one I would have asked for.

"We will have to move quickly," Dergoz says, the smile vanishing like the sun behind a cloud, all business once again. "Did the landing hurt you?"

"Huh?" I blink in confusion.

"You said that crash landing might damage your person. Are you all right?"

"Oh, yeah. Wait. Do you consider that a crash landing?"

He gestures around. "No. But now I am afraid for your delicate skin."

"Ah." I don't really know how to answer that. "Listen, I think it's probably better for you to be afraid to hurt me than accidentally get me killed, but you don't need to bundle me up in bubble wrap or anything. I'm tough."

"What is bubble wrap?"

"It's, like, a packing thing. To keep things intact when people, uh, take them long distances. It's filled with air to keep stuff from breaking."

"Perhaps I could make you garments out of this bubble wrap."

"That would definitely be a killer fashion statement," I say, laughing as I imagine Dergoz swathing me in a roll of plastic bubbles. "But it's not necessary. That's what I'm trying to tell you."

"I do not know. I rather like the idea of some kind of garment that will keep you free of injury."

I make a disgruntled noise, my eyebrows shooting up, until Dergoz surprises me with another gentle smile. "Wait, was that a joke?"

"No," he says seriously. "I never joke."

I squint at him. "I think it was a joke. I think you made a joke."

He shrugs one shoulder, looking adorably uncomfortable. "There are supplies in the crates in the back. Enough for both of us, I think, though I only have one temporary living quarter."

The webbing peels away again, and I stand shakily, my body adjusting the slight gravitational change of Nyria. "Temporary living quarters?"

"Yes. To sleep in? A temporary shelter?" He makes a vaguely triangular shape with his hands.

"Oh, like a tent." I shrug. "That's cool. We can share."

"Come," he tells me, and I blink at him, my entire body coming alive by that one word.

He inhales deeply, his diamond-pupil eyes dilating. "Your scent is distracting me."

"My scent?" My brows shoot up, and I tug my ponytail tighter as excitement winds through me. "Oh, shit, like you can scent that I'm turned on? I thought that was all made up. That's badass," I beam at him. Ooooh whee, if I can figure out my messed up emotions and enjoy the ride, it's gonna be a really, really good ride.

"It is intoxicating, and it is getting stronger." He frowns at me, like it's my fault.

My hands go to my hips. "I can't help it! You're talking sexy at me."

"The other warlords said their females hate when they say that." His frown deepens.

"Oh, you've got to be kidding me. So you got all filled in with guy gossip, but Niki and Gen shut down girl talk about your xof?" I wave a hand at him, still unsure where the hell it even is.

He steps closer, and a little thrill goes through me. "When you talk about my xof, it makes me want to throw you down against that chair and taste exactly where that scent is coming from."

I make an unintelligible sound.

The computer chimes, signaling another Roth ship incoming.

"We do not have time for me to pleasure you as a mate should be pleasured," Dergoz says, his eyes dark with promise. "So you shall continue to torture me with your sweet scent and tease me with your talk of my xof." With that, he stalks off, as though I'm doing it on purpose, leaving me gaping after him.

Well.

I grin wickedly at his retreating back. Maybe I *should* do it on purpose.

If we get clear of this ship, make it to our tent, maybe I will seduce him on purpose.

Because from the sounds of it, there's only one bed.

I laugh, and it's the kind that might give a villain a run for their money.

TWELVE

DERGOZ

THE FEMALE IS TESTING ME. I can tell from the wicked grin on her face, from the way her soft hands keep finding a way to touch me as we trek through the tall grass. Behind us, the ship's hidden in the grasses, though any cursory tech will find it immediately.

Still, Bex thought it best to leave an exit strategy intact, even if it means it will be crawling with Roth. She did, however, wipe the systems of anything that might lead them back to Sueva and our mission. To the Roth, it will appear as an abandoned cargo ship, one that experienced massive life support failure and filled to the brim with quickly souring fruit.

I could have done it, but Bex was so proud of herself that I could only stand back and watch.

"You did that more quickly than I would have," I tell her, still mulling it over.

She beams up at me, tracing her fingers along her bicep in a way that sends a shiver of desire through me. Sweat beads on her forehead, the heat of Nyria too much for her delicate constitution.

Still, she smiles at me, and it's like staring at the sun. Dazzling. And then there is that heady, delectable scent of hers, taunting me.

The grass comes up to my chin, allowing me to see over it, but poor petite Bex is walking blind.

I grab her hand, holding it in mine, distressed all over again about my mate being in this situation. Her skin is hot to the touch. Much warmer than usual.

"Is it too hot for you?"

She shrugs. "It's not great. I'll need water more often than normal, and to rest."

"It is *not* great," I agree. "It is bad. I will carry you when you grow weak. Suevan bodies are no stranger to extreme temperature differences. You should have told me before now. I will find this bubble wrap when we return to Sueva, if you continue withholding information from me."

This earns a snorted laugh from her, and I cannot help smiling at her yet again.

It feels so foreign, these grins she tugs from me, and yet, it also feels so incredibly right. I am so angry with myself for ignoring her these past few weeks, for letting one comment slip under my skin and poison my mind against her.

Something rustles in the grasses nearby, and I pull Bex against me, the back of her head flush against my pecs.

"What is that?" she whispers, her words barely audible. "I saw something huge… when we were landing."

"Local fauna," I say, uneasy. I do not know what lives on this moon. I know there are marine species on another planet in this system, but we have not made contact with them since our uneasy truce during the Settlement Wars against the Roth.

"It sounds bigger than fauna," she retorts, her small body tense against mine.

The grasses rustle again, and she smushes against me, her back pressing into my already hard cock. I stifle a groan, unbelievably aroused in spite of the precariousness of our situation.

Her delicious scent has changed though, to the bitter tang of fear. What kind of male am I, to think of making love to my mate when she is tense with fright?

"I will protect you," I say, bending down to whisper it in her ear. To my surprise, she shudders, then melts against me.

Could it be this is an erogenous zone for the human female?

The other warlords spoke of the things their humans liked, trading notes on how to best pleasure the female body, on how they can orgasm again and again if touched correctly while Alvez and I pretended not to listen in.

I do not remember them discussing the ears.

"Ree-becca," I whisper, testing my theory as my lips brush the soft shell of her ear. "I will keep you safe."

A throaty moan tears out of her, the fear-scent replaced by the intoxicating perfume of her arousal, despite the fact something huge and dangerous may stalk us, even now.

It seems the other warlords were correct about the insatiable nature of these human females.

It hardens my cock more than I could have ever believed possible, to think this little female will be slick with her desire at the mere touch of my lips against her ear.

I already grow addicted to the idea of it.

The sound draws nearer, and I slide the energy axe from where I've strapped it to my back. A reedy whine begins as the energy blade primes, and I hold it in front of us, clutching Bex with my other hand.

The thick grasses rustle again.

My eyes widen in surprise as the fearsome fauna appears.

"It's so fucking cute!" Bex screeches, holding her hand out and slipping from my grasp.

"Do not touch it," I warn her, but it's too late.

"It's a cat, oh my God, it's a baby," she says, crooning at the strange thing. It's not completely bad-looking as far as alien creatures go, the body covered in soft spotted fur. It's primarily a yellow green, but dark grey rosettes are sprinkled all over it.

It lets out a plaintive sound, fixing Bex with strange slitted pupils.

"What is a cat?" I ask, confused. "Is this an Earth animal?"

"It's a pet," she answers. "And no, *this* is not an Earth animal. But it looks a helluva lot like one, don't you, sweet baby cheetah thing?" she croons at it.

The animal mewls in response, rubbing its strange whiskered face along her hand. Whiskers! Of all the strange alien appendages. Only fish have whiskers on our planet.

I shudder at its oddness, slightly disgusted.

"Earth cats only have one tail," she adds, pointing at the six fluffed out tails behind it. "And this cat has extra toes. Seven, it looks like. I bet you are so good at climbing, huh? What a fierce little guy you are," she adds, using that high-pitched tone that the cat seems to love.

"We should keep moving and stop touching the wildlife. It might be poisonous." I want to yank her away from the strange and disgusting thing, but she just keeps petting it, even though now the thing is rumbling, a sound that strikes fear into my heart. "Why is making that noise?"

"It's purring!"

"Does that mean it will eat you?"

She shrugs. Shrugs!

"If it tries to eat you, I will kill it." My voice is low and menacing, and the foul cat's mouth pulls back, revealing hundreds of sharp teeth as it hisses a warning at me.

"Well, that's different, too," Bex says, amusement and apprehension flickering across her face.

"Your Earth cats do not have great maws of death needles?"

"Ah, no, they do, but they don't have quite so many."

"You keep creatures with deadly mouths as pets?"

"You make it sound so weird," she says.

I watch in horror as she scoops the creature up, cradling it close to her body. "What are you doing?"

"He needs a friend," she says.

"Oh no," I say, shaking my head, my mouth gaping in shock. "You cannot keep that monstrosity. Put it down."

She scratches under the cat's chin, it's six tails flicking back and forth frantically, the rumbling getting even louder. The hundreds of sharp needles glint near her face, and I'm frozen in fear for my mate.

"You should not let it's diseased teeth so near to your face," I whisper, afraid to agitate it further.

"Oh, you're a sweetie," she tells it, ignoring me completely. "Come on, Dergoz, let's go."

"You must put it down," I tell her.

"No," she says simply. "If he wants to get down, he'll let me know."

"That is exactly what I am afraid of, Ree-becca!"

"You wouldn't bite me, would you, kitty?"

I hold my breath as the thing rubs its cheek against her jawline, horrified. I still hold the energy axe in my hand, but I cannot move against the creature when she clings to it so firmly. I will just wound my mate, which is the exact outcome I seek to avoid.

"You cannot keep it!" I whisper-shout.

"Why not? Gen has a T-rex, Nikki has that weird thing with all the legs—"

"The zoleh is not a weird thing." I point to the six-tailed, whiskered monstrosity. "*That* is a weird thing."

"If it wants to go, it can go. Otherwise, it stays." With an infuriating shrug, she marches off through the thick grass, forcing me to jog after her to keep up.

Suddenly, the thick grass ends, and Bex gasps in horror.

The cat-creature leaps from her arms, wailing plaintively.

Fuck. Now I know she's going to want to keep it, no matter what.

BEX

I'M SO mad I can't see straight. A huge cat, twice as big as a lion, six tails limp on the scorched ground, lies before us. Dead.

The smaller cat prowls around it, nudging it with its head and making tragic whimpers.

"It's your mommy, isn't it, oh my God, you poor thing." I'm crying. I can't help it. "I used to rescue cats," I tell Dergoz. "On Earth, before the Roth, when I was in college, I fostered kittens and trapped ferals. It's a really heartbreaking thing to do, because so many of those babies are too sick to make it." I sniff. "But I've never seen anything like this."

The huge beast's fur is matted, dried blue-green liquid all along a huge hole in its head.

"That's a Roth pulse," Dergoz growls. "They killed it."

"AND I'LL FUCKING KILL THEM FOR IT!" I yell. Dergoz stares at me in alarm. The baby cat arches its back and hisses. "We're taking the damn cat with us."

"I know," Dergoz says wearily. "If it bites either one of us, we're not keeping it."

"It's not poisonous," I tell him, wiping my eyes with the back of my hand.

"You do not know that," he says, trepidation clear in his eyes. The cat rubs up against his legs, yowling. Slowly, he hooks the energy axe back in the sheath between his shoulder blades, sliding it neatly behind the huge backpack full of supplies he wears. It's super sexy, watching his muscles bunch, and I might stare for a bit longer than I need to.

"Why would the Roth kill your mommy?" I ask the cat, picking it up where it rubs against me.

"Probably because it is a very dangerous creature, with poisonous needle teeth and horrible whiskers."

I stare at him. "It's not poisonous. It's a cat."

"It is an alien," he says.

"So am I! So are you! That doesn't mean we're poisonous."

"No, but that does." Dergoz points to the dead creature's teeth, which are dripping a blue-black fluid.

"That could just be blood," I say hesitantly. The cat rubs its whiskered face against mine again, and I sigh in contentment. It smells like home, the familiar musky milk smell of kitten and feline fur. It makes me homesick, probably for the first time since we landed, and I bury my face in its back, overcome.

"Did it hurt you? Why are you making eye-water? The other warlords told me it happens when humans are distressed."

"You all are a bunch of miserable gossips," I manage, sniffling. The cat keeps purring.

"You must drink more water," Dergoz says, shoving a bottle at me. "You need your fluids in your body."

I take it, because he's right. I'm sweating profusely in the wicked heat of the planet, even the advanced camo fabric barely cooling me at this point. The water cools my throat, and I swallow greedily. The cat's claws dig into my shoulder as it readjusts, flopping its head against mine and hanging his paws over my back.

"Just a baby, just a widdle baby," I tell him, loving the familiar weight and the soothing purr.

"That thing is dangerous," Dergoz warns.

I narrow my eyes into slits. "So are we."

He sighs, and it's long-suffering. "Come, Bex, we must continue if we wish to make camp and rest this night."

I cuddle the cat, smiling over at Dergoz's scowling face. "Thank you," I tell him.

"For what?"

"For not arguing with me about the cat."

"I will not lie, Bex, I think this is a dangerous creature. But it brings a smile to your face, and for that, I will endure its loathsome appearance."

I bite my cheeks to keep from laughing. "Loathsome," I tell the cat. "You are beautiful, aren't you?"

Dergoz sighs again, and this time, I can't hold my laugh in.

"I'm sorry about your mommy," I tell the cat. "Don't worry, those bastards will get what's coming to them."

"That they will," Dergoz says, his tone bleak. "We agree on that, at least."

"Oh, come on, grumpy pants, we agree on lots of things." I fall in step with him, and he surprises me by brushing his fingers against my shoulder.

"What do we agree on?"

"Well," I say, putting a little more swing in my hips than is entirely necessary. "I think we both agree that we're going to find some things out about alien anatomy tonight."

"If you are suggesting I inspect the anatomy of that thing, you are very wrong."

I huff a laugh into the cat's soft fur. It mews, and I snuggle it even closer. "No, you big lump, I'm suggesting you inspect my anatomy."

"Oh," the syllable is a low growl, and his talons skate down my spine. "Now that, I could be convinced to do." Without another word, he scoops me up into his arms, and I readjust the weight of the alien cat to sit on my chest like a big furry baby.

"Thank you for letting me take the cat," I say softly, overwhelmed with a surge of affection towards the big alien.

"As if you would have listened if I said no," he says. "If I remember correctly, I did say no. Several times."

"Yeah," I admit, "but you're not fighting with me about it now or being rude. And I appreciate that."

"The foul creature is clearly somehow pleasing to you, despite the inherent danger of its sharp claws and too-many teeth. And whiskers," Dergoz adds, and he trembles. Trembles! As though the thought of the cat's whiskers are what sends the cat over the top into truly disgusting.

"We couldn't just leave him there. That was awful, what they did to his mother."

"It is always sad to see a great predator brought low, especially one with young," Dergoz grates out, as though admitting he has a squishy soft heart under those hard scales is a horrible thing. "It will not be easy to care for it on our mission, though. You could be endangering it further," he says softly, as though he is afraid of hurting my feelings.

He's afraid of hurting my feelings! He's carrying me around and he doesn't want to hurt my feelings!

I feel like I've won a prize, and I grin up at him, the weird-ass alien cat making biscuits with his too-many toes on my shoulder.

"If it wants to leave us, then I won't even to try to stop it. I don't know. I just feel like we have to try to take care of it." My nose scrunches up. Maybe my brains are muddled from the searing dry heat. It's not like me to get all irrational on a mission, because Dergoz is right. I'm more likely to get the little beastie murdered than save it.

Dergoz grunts, silence falling between us as he carries me steadily across the clearing, making a beeline for the shelter of strange trees branching high into the sky on the horizon.

"Perhaps it is the work of the many-faced goddess," Dergoz says finally.

I stare up at him, the cat beast asleep on my chest, purring softly. "What is?"

"The little creature. You said you felt compelled to bring it with us. To save it. The goddess works in strange ways."

"I didn't know you were religious."

"I do not know this word, *religious*." He stares down at me, puzzlement clear on his face.

"It's like," I cast around for the right word, unsure of how to describe it. "It's when people worship in a specific way, I guess. A specific god."

"There are no specifics when it comes to the many-faced goddess. She is beyond our comprehension. There is no right or wrong way to think about her." Dergoz's words are confused, and frankly, so am I.

"Cool," I say. "Sounds unproblematic, honestly." Religion's never been my thing, so at least I know settling in for the long haul with Dergoz won't mean waking up at zero dark thirty to do whatever Suevans do to worship.

Wait.

Wait.

Am I thinking about settling in for the long haul with Dergoz? Like, actually settling in… not just using him for a little stress relief and continuing hanging in the Bachelorette Tree Penthouse in Alien Paradise.

No. I shake my head.

"Your whole body has gone tight, my wife," Dergoz says, his eyes wide in alarm. "Are you overheating?"

"It's a little hot," I croak.

"It is this cat creature," Dergoz snarls, and the cat opens one eye lazily.

"No, it's not," I say. "I'm fine. Just hot."

Dergoz, however, doesn't seem to believe this for an instant, breaking into a run. He's not troubled by the weight of the pack he's slung across his back or the energy axe, like, not at all.

And now I'm up close and personal with the male I've been trying to get up close and personal to for weeks now, and I don't have a clue what to do with him.

Or what to do with my muddled-up emotions.

FOURTEEN

DERGOZ

IT TAKES me no time at all to set up the small portable living quarters. The PLQ will be tight with the two of us, but there is no way I am leaving my mate to sleep in it alone, not when she has said herself how fragile she is.

No, I will not be leaving her side, not for anything.

I dust my hands off on my pants, dragging the pack and our weapons inside the tent. It's immediately cooler on the inside, and satisfaction rolls through me.

Finally, I have a solution to help my Ree-becca.

"It is ready for you," I call.

Bex sweats under the shade of one of the knotty, bulbous trees, looking pale and listless as the cat-thing licks at her hand. I do not like that. I eye it warily.

"The alien cat is tasting you," I tell her.

"It's because I'm salty. I need to cool off." Her voice is slightly wispy, and I hate it. It's unpleasant for me, too hot here, on this dry planet, but my hide is much more suited to these conditions than her soft, soft skin.

"The cat-thing cannot come inside."

"His name is Horatio."

The cat-thing lets out a horrific wail, and I stare at it, waiting for it to attack.

"See? He's smart. He already knows his name." She presses a kiss to its ugly head, and it resumes licking her arm.

"Come," I tell her. "Leave the cat." I grab her by the elbow, helping her stand, then loop my arm around her waist and pull her towards the PLQ.

"I can walk," she says. "But I'm not going to argue."

The cat-thing, Horatio, follows her, its six tails jauntily waving in the air.

"There is no room for you inside," I tell it, then immediately feel foolish for talking to the thing. It yips a reply that I cannot make heads or tails of, then settles outside, in the shade of the PLQ.

"See?" Bex says loftily. "He understands."

"He knows I will not tolerate him inside," I growl.

Horatio slowly blinks at me.

I narrow my eyes at it, then help Bex inside.

It's much darker in the tent, and Bex immediately sighs in relief as the cooler air gusts over her. "God, it's got to be one-twenty out there."

"Water," I tell her, concern growing as she buries her face in her hands.

She takes the bottle from me, sipping slowly, and I settle next to her, watching her throat bob. It's not enough.

I stand again, digging out a small square cloth from the pack. I hold my hand out, and Bex passes the bottle back to me. A drip is all it takes, and the square quintuples in size, frost coating it. The air around it crystallizes in the sudden temperature drop, fogging it.

"Ooh," Bex says appreciatively, and my cock immediately hardens at the sheer desire in her voice. Not for me, but for the cool cloth.

And I did that. I made her make that small noise.

"Drink more," I tell her. "Lie back. I will attend to you." My voice is gruff, and to my surprise, she doesn't argue.

Which is either a sign of how distressed her delicate human system is, or a sign that she trusts me.

I hope it is the latter, though I am not sure what I could have possibly done to have earned her trust after my abysmal treatment of her, after all the assumptions I made about the kind of female she was.

Carefully, I draw her damp tail of hair away from her neck, pushing loose strands behind her ears, then gingerly wiping the sweat and dirt from her beautiful face. Her lips part, and she sucks in a breath.

I catalogue every small change in her expression, filing it away, wanting to see them all, to collect them and put them on display in my heart.

Satisfied that her face is clean, pleased with the normal tone of her skin returning, I move lower, to her neck, and she shivers at the touch.

"Is it too cold?" I ask, alarmed at her body's response.

"Keep going," she says, her voice husky.

I squeeze my eyes shut, my breathing uneven. I should not desire her so much, not when she is in need and veering towards being unwell.

And yet I lust for her, undone by the smallest changes in her mouth, in the cast of her eyes, which now pin me in place, dark and mysterious.

I return to my task, savoring it as a true husband might. A true mate.

There is a dip in the base of her throat, and I drag the cloth over it, making sure that it is clean and free of sweat. That she is cooling off.

On an impulse, I press a kiss to it, unable to stop myself from luxuriating in the taste of her sweat, of her sweet skin. A low whimper comes from her, and I stop, jerking back.

"I have gone too far," I say, shaking my head, shame filling me.

"No," she whispers, and when I open my eyes, I see hers are full of desire. The sweet scent of her arousal fills the PLQ. "Keep going."

A low growl leaves my throat, surprising me. Her small fingers circle my wrists, and she moves my hands, forcing them under the camo tech fabric. I groan. Desire whips me, and yet I stop myself from delving further, from exploring the bounty of her body.

Not yet. I want her to be clean and comfortable and cool.

Then? Then I will *devour* her.

BEX

I HAVE NEVER BEEN SO GODDAMN TURNED on in my entire life. The alien tent is more like a temporary tiny home, all futuristic and metallic and blessedly cool.

I can hardly focus on it.

All I can focus on is the cold, damp cloth. On Dergoz, stroking it gently, reverently, over my skin.

It feels like heaven. It feels like being pampered, like being at the spa or something—but it's so much more.

Because I've never once had anyone look at me the way Dergoz does, with both trepidation and a desire so fierce that it takes my breath away. Like I'm the only thing he can see.

Right now, he's literally all I can see, his huge green bulk taking up all the space in the tent, taking up all the air. My breathing's turned heavier now, faster, as he works the cloth across my bare arms, sopping up all the sweat and dirt.

He wrings the cloth out, then trickles a little fresh water onto it again, and a cloud of frost forms around it.

It's some seriously cool tech, and part of me can't wait to

figure out how, exactly, it works. The other part can't wait to see where else Dergoz is going to put it.

I shuck my shirt, my chest heaving, and my sports bra feels more intimate than the lingerie I fell asleep in only a day ago. Especially with the way he looks at me in it, like all his dreams came true all at once.

Still, he doesn't move, just watches me watch him.

"Well?" I finally ask, barely recognizing my own husky voice.

"You are more than I ever… You are perfect."

My heart squeezes, a fresh surge of affection rolling through me. I'm not perfect. But I almost believe him, the way he looks at me so full of longing it makes me feel… sad. Because if I hadn't let my stupid mouth get away from me when we first met, I wouldn't have fucked all this up between us.

"I'm sorry I hurt you," I say, sitting up, clutching the shirt to my chest.

"What? You have not hurt me," Dergoz says, confusion written all over his adorable face. His tail swishes, banging against the hard shell of the Suevan tent.

"I mean, your feelings. I'm sorry that you thought I was calling you… a monster." Impulsively, I reach a hand out, cupping the smooth scales on his cheek. "You aren't a monster. You have never been a monster. It was a stupid thing to say, and it had nothing to do with who you are, and had everything to do with who I am."

"Ree-becca," Dergoz says, his gaze darting away from me, landing on the frosty cloth in his hand. "I have done many things that are monstrous. You are not wrong about that."

"That isn't what I meant," I sigh. "It's juvenile, but listen, okay? The monster thing… It's because of books I read. Books I love." My nose wrinkles, because, damn, does this sound stupid. "In them, the women get together with, er—" I pick my words carefully. "—nonhuman creatures, and they have bangin' sex, and they fall in love. It's a fantasy. These dudes, the males, you know, the, er, nonhuman partners, they always treat the women like gold and give them orgasm after orgasm and I've never met any human man that does that. Ever." I shake my head for emphasis.

Dergoz just stares at me as though I've grown whiskers like sweet Horatio snoozing outside the tent.

"So you call these males, who give their women pleasure and treat them well… monsters."

"Ah, sure!" I say, a bit too brightly, and he frowns at me. "Okay, that's not really what it means. But the thing about monsters in these books, and that's what I was talking about, just to remind you, is that no matter how different they look, they are good inside. They are worthy of love."

"Then I will be your monster, my Ree-becca," Dergoz tells me. "I will be worthy of your love."

It's so sweet. It's just so damn sweet, and I blink up at him, wondering if he'll kiss me again, wanting him to kiss me again.

Wanting him. All of him.

And he just smiles gently down at me, stroking the cold cloth over the curves of my shoulders, over the tops of my breasts.

Doing it so slowly, so patiently and carefully, that it makes me like him even more.

"I am sorry, too," he finally says. "I am sorry I have pushed you away when we could have had this conversation weeks ago. I am stubborn and set in my ways."

"That makes two of us," I manage, shivering in anticipation as the cloth edges lower, across my stomach, towards the pants that molded themselves to my much, much smaller frame.

"Take them off," he says.

I immediately get wet, everything between my legs tightening, lust darts through me, and his diamond-pupils dilate in response.

"Why are your eyes doing that?" I ask, knowing the answer, but wanting him to say it anyway.

"Because I can scent your arousal, female, and it is driving me insane."

"What are you going to do about it?" I ask. I want him insane. I want him. Period.

To my surprise, he sits back, sighing deeply.

"I should tell you something about myself," he says.

I blink, some of my lust ebbing. This doesn't sound good. "Uh, okay. Hit me with it."

His jaw drops, his tail flicking furiously behind him. "I would never hit you, Ree-becca."

I haven't let anyone else call me Rebecca in years. But I like when he says it. I shake my head, swallowing a laugh.

"That's not what that means. It means, uh, tell me what is on your mind."

"I am not good with females. I do not have the experience of some of the others."

I sit up in surprise. Of all the confessions, this is not the one I was expecting. But it makes sense, kind of. On why he refused to even look at me.

"You're a virgin," I manage, astonished. "Why didn't you tell me you've never had sex?"

"I am not untried." He sniffs. "I have had sex."

"Then what are you worried about?" I narrow my eyes. Maybe he's into weird shit. I could be into weird shit. Most weird shit. Maybe shit isn't the right term at the moment.

"The one female I was with, ten years ago… she laughed afterwards." His huge, capable body is tense with awkwardness, and I blink up at him.

"She laughed at you… the one female. The woman who took your virginity laughed at you?"

"I have not been with a female since."

I sink back, letting his confession wash over me. No wonder he didn't trust me. No wonder he's been cagey and stubborn and weird.

"You are upset," he says.

"No, not at all." I jerk back up, succeeding in smashing my forehead into his. "Unf," I grunt, rubbing between my brows.

"I am sorry, my Ree-becca, I did not expect you to headbutt me."

"Same. Okay, Dergoz." I squint, then take the cold cloth from his hands, placing it on the new achy spot on my eyebrow. "Whoever it was you slept with, she sucked."

"No, she did not do that. She did not have a chance," he says sadly.

I squeeze my eyes shut. *Don't laugh, don't laugh.*

"No," I gasp out, my voice weird and tight. "I meant she was a bad person. A bad alien. That was mean of her."

"I came too soon. I did not give her pleasure." His voice is anguished, raw, and it's clear this has troubled him for a long time.

"Hey, that's okay."

"It does not bother you?" He stares at me, as though expecting me to yell at him or something.

"Why would it? Lots of dudes finish early. It's about practice." I give him a meaningful look. "Stamina. Would you expect one of your trainees, wannabe whatever Suevan Warlords to be able to last as long in the fighting ring as say, you or Draz?"

"Of course not." He snorts with laughter, the idea clearly absurd. "We'd lay them out flat in a matter of minutes."

I raise my eyebrows.

Understanding dawns in his eyes. "Oh. Oh. I never thought of it like that."

"It's all about practice, Dergoz, and having a patient partner." I shrug, tugging at the cool cloth in his hand. If he's too shy to continue, I'm going to wash myself, that thing feels too good to just let it go to waste.

He snatches it out of reach, something firing in his eyes. "And you want to be my patient partner," he says quietly, the question implicit.

"Obviously," I say, "but to be honest, I'm not feeling very patient right now."

"You are impatient... for my cock."

I make a strangled noise, still trying to tug the cold cloth from his hands. "I mean, I just wanted to get clean at the moment—"

"Your scent is all over the air." He inhales deeply. "Why are you lying now, about wanting my cock deep inside you?" His head tilts, his tail lashing from side to side.

My eyes go wide.

"You tell me you want to be my patient partner, and then you perfume the air with your sex scent, which is driving me..." He grits his teeth, his fangs pressing on his lower lip. "Insane. And then you tell me you want to get clean only. Is this the human way? To say one thing and mean another?"

I blink. He thinks I'm playing games?

"Okay, I'm not playing games."

"I did not say you were playing games." He sniffs. "We do not have any games. At no point have we played games."

"I'm not talking about Monopoly, Dergoz." I exhale, trying to collect my thoughts. And I am turned on, dammit, it would be hard not to be, with all that muscled male touching me.

"I do not know this word," he says, shaking his head, frustration clear in his eyes.

"What, you all don't have a tiny dude in a top hat and tails trying to teach you to prioritize the joy of capitalism over your friendships while you push tiny shiny toys around a square piece of cardboard?"

He stares at me in confusion. "Humans have strange ways."

I clear my throat, letting my hand fall away from the cloth. "Okay, here's the thing, Dergoz. I'm going to level with you, because you came clean to me."

"I am not clean. I am cleaning you first."

I stare at the ceiling for a beat, gathering myself. You'd think now that we can actually understand each other, communication would be easier.

"I meant you opened up to me. Told me what was on your mind. So now, it's my turn to tell you something about me."

He sits back a little, a speculative look in his eyes.

"I am not good at… relationships. I am good at sex, but I'm not good at… letting people get to know the real me." My throat closes up, and I cough. Alarm flares across Dergoz's face.

"Are you sick? Has this planet made you ill?"

"No," I say, "I seemed to forget how to swallow there for a minute."

His expression grows increasingly concerned.

"I'm fine," I assure him, but my brain is still flailing around. "This is just hard for me to talk about. It's easy to make jokes, and be ridiculous, and over-the-top… but it's hard for me to… you know—"

"To talk about how much you love me already," Dergoz finishes.

Taken aback, I stare at him open-mouthed. "What?"

"It is hard for you to admit that you are obsessed with me, my cock, my xof—" He punctuates this remark by grabbing himself. "—my heart. I understand. Love can be a frightening concept. But I am ready to admit that my feelings for you are growing by the hour. And my cock is growing even more rapidly."

Stunned, I simply blink at him, my gaze darting between his honest, open expression and where his hand rests on the bulge between his legs.

"I—"

"Do not worry, my petite meat blanket—"

"Your what?!"

He frowns, then a smile slowly spreads across his face. "Is this not a term humans use? This is the sweetest of all Suevan phrases. For I will bury my cock in you, and your cunt will wrap around me like the most beautiful of all—"

"Nope!" I yelp. I hold up a hand, squeezing my eyes shut, like that's going to block out the mental image he's painting too easily for me. *Meat blanket.* Jesus Christ. I'm starting to see why the other woman he had sex with laughed, if this is his idea of sexy time talk. His earnest enthusiasm is endearing, but arousing it is *not*.

I have my work cut out for me.

Good thing I'm more than up to the challenge.

I exhale through my nose, trying to muster up the courage to say what needs to be said.

When I open my eyes, Dergoz is watching me through narrowed eyes, as if waiting for the verbal blow to fall.

"Okay." I press my lips together, sorting through my thoughts. "So, sex is about finding out what your partner likes, and what you can do to please them, okay?"

"You will be my only partner for the rest of my existence," Dergoz announces, and I raise my eyebrows.

I ignore the little flutter in my stomach. *One thing at a time.*

"Right. Then we need to figure out what we both like. And I do not, under any circumstances—" I wince, the words not even wanting to come out of my mouth. "—want to be called a meat blanket. Ever again. Please."

He nods seriously. "If that is what it will take to fill our PLQ with the scent of your arousal, I will not call you meat blank—"

"Don't even say it," I interrupt. "Okay. So, I also like when you tell me what you want to do with me. That turns me on."

He blinks. "You have a switch?"

Exasperated, I pinch the bridge of my nose. "No, it's a human expression. I mean it arouses me, when you tell me—"

"That I want to lick and suck at your cunt until you scream my name and your sweet honey fills my mouth?"

I cough again. "That would do it. But this goes both ways. So what do you like?"

He inches closer, his expression serious, lust flaring in his eyes. "I would like to taste you. Every sound you make triggers my switch."

"Triggers your—oh."

He wants to dive straight into oral. I mean, who am I to say no to that?

"I want to kiss your lips," he says. "I want to put my tongue in your mouth."

My nose wrinkles. "We'll work on the talk. But yes. I would like you to kiss me, too."

It's all I need to say before his lips are on mine again, his strange textured tongue swiping into my mouth, stealing my breath. His hand strokes across the exposed skin of my stomach, and I relax into his slow, soothing rhythm.

His huge body traps mine beneath him, muscled arms caging me in as he lowers me to the inflatable pallet that somehow was already inside his tent.

God, he feels amazing, so strong.

He breaks off the kiss, and I make a small, involuntary whimper as the warmth of his mouth leaves mine.

"That is the noise I want, Ree-becca," he says roughly, and the way he says my name drives me crazy.

"I like when you call me that," I tell him, my voice low and husky, and he smirks down at me.

"I know. I can tell exactly what you like."

And if that's not the hottest, bossiest thing anyone has ever said to me in bed.

"Now I will find out what else makes your beautiful eyes shutter with pleasure and the pretty moans come from your mouth. I am going to kiss you all over, work my tongue over your folds until you are slick with arousal and begging me for more."

He tilts his head, studying me. My breath's coming faster now.

"Was that better sex talk?"

"It was perfect," I tell him. "I would like that very much." I nod my head enthusiastically.

His tail lashes back and forth, a proud smile appearing on his face. Then his mouth dips to my sports bra, and he tugs at the peak of my nipple with his teeth, his fangs bookending it.

I arch off the ground, my fingers scrabbling along his shoulders. He growls, and it just makes me even hotter. I push the band of the sports bra up, tugging it over head and then lie back, staring up at him.

"These are…" He shakes his head. "Words fail me. You are the most beautiful, confusing creature I have ever met."

His tongue darts out, and he licks a circle around my nipple. My hands thread through his hair, and I moan, getting wetter by the second. That tongue on my skin… it is so. Fucking. Good.

"You like this," he says, his voice full of wonder, so sweet that my heart does that little squeeze again.

"I like that," I agree.

When he dips his head to my other breast, repeating the motion, I shiver with need, my legs starting to shake as everything in me begins to beg for release.

"You like it very much," he says, then gently teases the tip of my nipple with his teeth, causing me to cry out.

"I like it," I agree, my voice high and needy.

"I like it, too," he says roughly. "My xof already begins to sing for you."

I scrunch my nose up, confusion rocketing through me. "Begins to what?"

Instead of answering, though, he grabs my hand, pressing it to the massive bulge in his pants.

My eyes go wide.

He's vibrating.

"It vibrates?" My tone is gleeful. *Oh, shit yeah.* This is going to be so. Much. Fun.

"Yes, my xof vibrates, it sings for you." He stares down at me with an awed expression that makes my stomach explode into happy butterflies. "The only way Suevan females can procreate is after they have their annual orgasm."

"Annual?!"

"Do not worry, my Ree-becca," he says, licking my nipple again, eyes fixed on mine. "The other warlords told me human females can come many, many times, and I am eager to see how many orgasms I can force from you."

"Oh," I say, relaxing again.

His fingers slip down my body, unfastening and tugging down

my pants, a harsh growl escaping him again, ratcheting my desire even higher. One hand delves between my legs, and I follow his gentle touch, pressing my hips up against his hand, chasing the pressure.

"Your cunt is already soaked for me," he says, and when he brings his fingers to his lips, I moan again.

"That feels good," I tell him.

"Then lie still and let me pleasure you. Let me be in charge of your body," he commands, and I stare up at him, loving this transformation. It's like all my naughty dreams are coming true at once. "You like when I am in control," he says, his lip curling in satisfaction. "Your readiness proves it."

I arch an eyebrow, curious how far he's going to take this, reaching down between our bodies to see exactly what he's packing. Exactly what my new favorite vibrator looks and feels like.

"No," he grits out, as my fingertips brush his hardness. "This is about your pleasure. Your pleasure brings me pleasure." He catches my wrist, pinning it on the side of my hip.

I squirm, incredibly excited, practically panting.

Slowly, languidly, like we have all the time in the world, he sits back, staring at me, drinking me in.

"Beautiful," he rasps, then yanks my pants off the rest of the way, roughly tugging my underwear to the side.

He groans, eyes shutting as he inhales deeply, and everything coils tight inside me, preparing for what he's about to do.

A split-second later, I find out.

CHAPTER
SIXTEEN

DERGOZ

I NEVER EXPECTED THIS FEMALE. I never expected the dark thatch of curls hiding her cunt from me, nor the spectacular perfume of it, or the incredible taste of her as I lap at her place of pleasure.

"Oh, Dergoz, right there, right there," she pants, and I chase her movements with my mouth, flicking my tongue across the bud of her pleasure as she squeals and moans.

I am so hard that precum wets the tops of my trousers, lost in the taste and silken slide of her across my mouth.

"So fucking right," I say savagely, then suck at the small bud she seems to prefer I pay attention to. She nearly jumps off the floor, her chest heaving.

"Dergoz," she whimpers, "that's it. That was so good. So good."

I want more. I'm not done. I want to know all the ways to pleasure my small, dainty, luscious human. I want to explore all of her.

I have never been so hard in my entire life.

Growling, I snap off two talons from my fingers, and her eyes widen as she realizes what I'm going to do.

"That is right, my Ree-becca. I am going to fuck your cunt with my fingers now, and see how ready you truly are for me. I am going to feast on this wetness, do you understand?"

She nods, her expression dazed, her cheeks flushed from the power of her first orgasm. I would give her a thousand. I would pleasure her all night, just to see the amazement in her eyes again and again.

I am already addicted to this.

Slowly, I press my mouth back between her legs, my eyes closing as I grind my hips into the floor. She's moaning, bucking beneath me, and I lock my arm around her lower back, spreading her soft thighs even further apart.

I love watching her almost as much as I love the taste of her in my mouth.

Carefully, I run my finger around her opening, savoring the way she feels before plunging it inside her.

"Oh, oh my God, oh my God," she whines, her head thrown back. Her blunt fingernails scrape against my scalp, the sensation and her need driving me further into desire.

Her cunt clenches around my finger, and I thrust the second inside, licking her all the while.

It doesn't take her long at all to come again, and I smile as the sounds of her pleasure fill the tent. My eyes squeeze shut, and I grit my teeth, my own release not far away.

"Dergoz," she says, in a tender tone I have not yet heard from her. "I can't anymore. I need to sleep. Here." She moves positions suddenly, and as soon as her hand brushes against my cock, I explode, the force of my own orgasm soaking my pants.

I shudder, shame and relief warring for purchase.

"Oh," she says. "That's okay. Hey, don't worry about it. Did it feel good? Did you like it?"

"I fucking loved it," I grate out, then I stare at her in wonder. "You are incredible."

I grab the cleansing cloth, making sure to tend to her first while she smiles sleepily up at me. By the time I have cleaned myself and taken my own pants off, she's half asleep.

She is so peaceful like this.

Gently, so as not to fully wake her, I curl up next to her, gathering her into my arms.

She is more precious to me already than I ever could have imagined.

And tomorrow I must take her into danger.

SEVENTEEN

BEX

I WAKE UP HAPPY.

For the first time in years, I feel light, and refreshed, and fully at ease.

A hard object presses into my lower back, and my eyes fly completely open. Dergoz's arm is slung around my waist, another under my head, acting as a scaly pillow. He's perfectly warm and smooth, not at all sweaty or gross like some of the men I've woken up to in the past.

I usually hate cuddling.

Despise it.

Which, according to the old therapist I saw on Earth, is a sign that I use sex to feel connected to someone instead of using actual, well, connections. One side of my mouth scrunches up. Those weren't her exact words, but it's close enough to the sentiment.

Except… in Dergoz's arms… I don't want to shove him off or push him out the door and throw his stupid loafers at his face.

Not that he even would know what a loafer is, which might be a big part of his appeal.

I love that he's different.

I love that last night… it was all about me. And he didn't make me feel selfish or needy.

He just… did it because it brought him pleasure, too.

"Good morning, my little ray of sunshine." He presses a kiss behind my ear, scooting me closer to him.

"Hi," I say, ignoring the way I'm grinning like an idiot at his term of endearment. Much better than meat blanket.

"Did you sleep well? Today is going to be another long hike, I fear." He kisses all along my neck, and a shiver runs through me, my cheeks hurting from smiling.

Dergoz pulls me even closer, his cock and xof vibrating all along my back. It's an alien dick massage, and I never even thought about that being a thing until now.

I have the most insane urge to open my mouth and sing a note, just to see if it gives me a vibrato, but I clamp down on it, instead nestling deeper into his shoulder.

"What are you thinking about?" he asks, his nose pressed into the top of my head.

"Dolly Parton's hit song, 'Nine To Five'," I say automatically.

"Human musicians write songs about arithmetic?" he asks, running his fingers along the curve of my side. "How strange."

"Ah, sometimes," I finally answer, at a loss and not in the mood to even try to explain that. I just want to lay here, in quiet bliss, without overanalyzing what any of this means, as long as I can.

Of course, Dergoz immediately stretches long, so tall the tips of his fingers and toes hit the ends of the hard-shell tent. He stands, and I roll onto my back, admiring the view.

Damn. He's just… so built? It's the kind of a muscle a human man would have to work for decades to achieve, and probably also use illegal substances that would make sure their dicks never sang again.

"You have a strange look on your face."

"I do?" I pat my cheeks, like that will tell me what my face will look like. "Ouch. I think I got a sunburn yesterday."

"That is not good," Dergoz intones, a dangerous edge to his voice. He crouches in front of me, inspecting my face. "You will wear something to block the sun today."

It's so gosh darn sweet, the way he wants to take care of me. "You have sunblock?"

"We will fashion one out of one of my camo tech shirts."

"Oh," I say. He literally means to block the sun. That's fine. "What about you?"

He stares at me. "I have a scaled hide."

"Right."

"I would trade all my scales if it meant making you more comfortable."

"Dergoz, that's unnecessary," I say, squirming slightly as he tugs a clean pair of pants on. Thank goodness he had a spare, because one look at his pants from last night tells me they're not gonna be wearable until they get a nice, thorough soak. And possible decontamination.

"It is necessary. After what you told me last night, about how you have trouble with relationships, I will not be able to do anything but ensure that you are as comfortable, as safe, and as protected as possible. And that you come at least five times a night."

My eyebrows raise up. I tilt my chin to the side, completely at a loss for what to say. "Five times?"

"Yes. At least five to nine, like your human musicians sing about. I take it this is a sacred number for your people?"

"Ah, the song is nine to five, but it doesn't matter. And I guess some people probably do consider the nine to five sacred." I shrug a shoulder, trying to ignore the way my heart's skipping around, telling me he's going too fast. That this is too fast.

Forget nine to five, the Suevan Brute is zero to sixty.

I sink back to the floor of the tent, staring at the tiny apertures letting in light and air all over the ceiling.

They warned me. All the girls warned me that these males are in it to win it. Hell, I'm already married to the guy, and I'm still freaked out by how suddenly he's all in.

Fuck.

I love the chase. I love sex.

I'm not good at love. I'm bad at this.

I squeeze my eyes shut, trying to pull the reins on my runaway heartbeat. I just need to take this one day at a time. Enjoy the ride. See what happens.

No sooner has the thought filtered through my brain than I feel Dergoz's hot breath between my legs.

"I think we should start the morning with your first orgasm," he announces.

"Okay," I breathe, my eyes wide.

Maybe I should just take it one orgasm at a time.

CHAPTER
EIGHTEEN

DERGOZ

I AM WELL PLEASED. My human wife saunters alongside me, her tiny legs stepping twice as quick for every one of mine. The horrible feline alien, Horatio, to my eternal dismay, appears to have also slept well, rubbing contentedly all along our legs.

"Does he seem larger today?" I ask Bex, squinting at the many-tailed beast.

"He's a growing boy," she responds, using that baby voice she adopts when she speaks to the foul thing.

"I suppose," I say, eyeing it warily.

The cat makes a mewling noise, rubbing its whiskered cheek all along my knee. The thing is decidedly larger. An odor emits where he strokes my legs, and I grimace, trying to shake it off.

"Why does it release its smell on us?"

Bex claps her hands delightedly, only her eyes visible through the cloth I've wound around her pretty face. "He's marking us! That means he thinks we're his. Awww, what a sweet boy."

I grumble, but secretly, I love seeing how pleased she is with the disgusting furred creature. She has such a sweet, soft heart.

Everything about her is like that, too, soft and sweet and so fucking delectable.

"I cannot wait to set the PLQ up for the night. I already want you again," I tell her fiercely.

"Well," she says wryly, her eyes dipping to the front of my trousers, "you're already pitching a tent."

My tail swings back and forth as I try to decipher her words.

"Your pants… you know what? Never mind." She peels back more of the packet around the meal replacement bar she's chewing on, taking another big bite.

The sun is not as hot overhead yet today, and for that I am thankful. The sky is a light blue, nearly green, and seems empty compared to the asteroid dotted Suevan horizon. Bex soaks in the Nyrian biome with avid interest, pointing out the odd trees and animals with clear fascination.

Horatio scampers off more than once, only to return with his maw covered in blood and to have Bex coo over him.

I check the comms tablet, using it to track the location Nydo gave up as the entrance to the underground facility. According to his intel, we're still a few hours walk from it.

I do not want to take my mate into the data storage facility. I do not want to walk her straight into danger.

The ground rumbles under my feet, and Bex's hand darts out, grasping my wrist for support. Her brown eyes are wide.

"Is it an earthquake?"

I squint at the horizon, where a huge, dark cloud races towards us.

"I do not think it is," I tell her, jerking my head towards the mass in the air.

Underfoot, the ground continues to quake.

"It's a stampede," Bex says, her fingers tight on my arm. "Look," she says, pointing at the cloud.

A mass of writhing animal bodies tears towards us, the ground shaking as the alien creatures hammer their way across the grassland. Their legs are long and spindly, but there are enough of them to flatten the grass beneath their yellow-green hooves.

Horatio lets out a plaintive yowl that sounds somewhat like he's screaming yes at the beasts. I narrow my eyes at the strange, hideous creature.

"Oh, God." Bex's voice is barely audible over the sound of approaching hooves. "They're headed straight for us. We're going to be trampled."

Her assessment is correct.

In one smooth motion, I pull the energy axe from the sheath between my shoulder blades. Bex seems frozen in place, her eyes huge and dark in her face.

"Get behind me," I yell at her, tugging her wrist to jerk her into action.

"Shouldn't we just run for it?" she shouts back. "I don't think this is the best course of action."

"We won't be able to outrun them. There are too many. Look how wide the herd stretches."

"Fuck."

I don't hear her as much as I mark the shape of her mouth as it makes the word.

Horatio rubs his foul face against my calf, and I lash my tail behind me before forcibly yanking my mate behind the shield of my body. I am unsure that it will be enough, and terror consumes me.

I am unsure that I, the Brute of Sueva, will be enough to save her from the mindless onslaught of the stampeding beasts.

My eyes squeeze shut as I attempt to gather my thoughts, to quell the rising panic at the thought of losing her to a herd of alien herbivores.

"We just need to be scarier than whatever's chasing them," Bex shouts, her hand tugging at my shoulder. "Something spooked them into their stampede, so we need to make it worth their while to turn back."

"It is a good plan," I manage. The beasts are so close now that their stench fills the air, a musky animal scent tinged with the bitter edge of fear.

"What do you think is chasing them?" Bex asks, and this time, her nails bite into my shoulder.

"We do not want to find out," I yell back.

Horatio winds between my legs, his tails coming into uncomfortable proximity to my upper thighs. I swat him away, only managing to get my hand tangled in one of his tails. The creature blinks up at me, his rows of needle-sharp teeth too close to my favorite body part for comfort.

I cannot say I am the beast's biggest fan.

"Horatio," Bex calls out, "go run, little buddy! Save yourself! You can outrun them, I bet!"

Sighing, I make a split-second decision. "Come, horrible animal, jump onto my shoulder. I will not have my mate saddened because of your untimely demise."

But the disgusting thing simply opens its mouth wider, showing more of its decidedly unsettling teeth. I cringe away instinctively, holding the energy axe with both hands in case the thing decides to make a meal of me.

Instead, Horatio lets out an ear-shattering scream, the likes of which I have never heard before in my life and hope never to hear again.

It's long and loud and impossibly high pitched, sending a chill down my spine as the feline's mouth gapes wider than it should.

Horatio bounds off towards the approaching herd, and I drop the axe, clapping my hands over my ears as he continues his terrible song.

Bex leans against my back, her hands over her own ears, the screaming alien creature racing towards the stampede. I tug her into my chest, more worried about her sensitive human hearing than my own, trying to protect her from the wretched noise that seems to short-circuit all my brain function.

There is no sound of hooves, no background white noise whatsoever, only the endless scream of the horrible alien Bex decided to attach herself to as a pet.

Nightmares of its teeth will likely plague me the rest of my life.

We stand like that for too long, the axe forgotten on the ground. The only thing that matters is blocking out the horrible sound of the demon alien cat and protecting Bex from whatever it is doing to scramble all of my senses so thoroughly.

She shifts against me, and it takes me a moment to realize she's shoving my shoulder, pointing.

"Look," she mouths, and I blink, realizing that I cannot hear her. I scrub at my ears, trying to gain more hearing besides the dull ringing that drowns everything else out. It sounds as though she speaks to me underwater.

She points again, aggressively, her mouth round with shock. I follow the direction of her fingers, my heart slamming against my chest, my tail shaking slightly as adrenaline leaves my body.

The cat—Horatio—stands between us and the herd, the animals fleeing in terror before him. He's still screaming, high pitched yelping, turning the ungulates away from my mate.

Away from me.

The wretched furred animal saved my mate.

Gratitude fills me, and I inhale deeply. "The hand of the goddess is on this," I say solemnly, looking to where I know Sueva sits in space, far, far, away. My own voice sounds equally far away.

"Horatio," Bex calls out, crouching down and patting her knees. The alien cat, our unexpected savior, bounds towards her, tails held high like he knows exactly what he just did and wants all the praise in the galaxy. She scoops Horatio up, planting a kiss on his furry forehead, and I am not even jealous.

I, too, would kiss his foul little furry face, as a thanks for keeping my mate safe.

"See?" she says, scratching around his loathsome whiskers. "He's meant to be with us. He has to stay with us." Fat drops of water roll down her cheeks, and concern fills me as I stare at the cloudless blue sky.

"You are leaking from your eyes in distress."

"I'm crying." She sniffs. "It's normal. I'm overwhelmed. That was… one of the most terrifying things that's happened to me in a long, long time. Probably since the Roth invasion."

Thank the goddess, I can understand her. My ears still ring, but they recover every moment. Carefully, I wrap my arms around her, the alien cat between us. She shudders, the eye-water continuing.

"You are safe now. We are safe now, thanks to your—" My tongue stumbles over the strange name. "Horatio."

The cat makes a loud yowling sound, as though in agreement with my assessment. I narrow my eyes at the beast. Surely it is not intelligent enough to understand our foreign words. That would be impossible.

It should be impossible, at any rate.

I hold her for longer than I should, relief and gratitude at Horatio saving her from the herd of alien hoofed beasts momentarily making me forget our pressing need to find the Roth bunker.

"We should move," I finally say, my tiny mate's breathing deep and even, the cat butting his head against her face, likely looking for more kisses, the greedy beast.

"Okay," she agrees, sniffling. Her nose is pink, and she swipes at it with the back of her hand.

I need to find a way to get her spaceside again immediately. I hate that she is in danger because of me.

As soon as we find the Roth base, I will commandeer her a ship and force her off planet. I will not risk my one chance at happiness at the hands of the Roth.

"You have a weird look in your eyes," she says suspiciously.

I blink slowly. "Is it gone now?"

She snorts. "Nevermind." Smiling, she reaches out for my hand, and I take it.

I will not feel guilty for wanting to keep my mate safe. I will not feel guilty for doing anything necessary to make her so.

I will not feel guilty for clutching at my own happiness.

Keeping her safe is the right thing to do.

"You sure nothing is bothering you?" she asks again, shading her eyes against the sun as she stares up at me.

"Other than my ears ringing from the cat, no. I am glad that we evaded those hooved creatures." And I am.

And I will do everything in my power to make sure that she never has to stare death down in the face again. A plan to keep her safe forms in my head, and I cling to it like it is a rock on a flooding Suevan mountainside.

CHAPTER
NINETEEN

BEX

DERGOZ IS ACTING STRANGELY. He's happy. Too happy, especially considering we nearly were trampled to death by a rampaging herd of strange antelope-like creatures.

He's downright chipper.

I try to be a positive person, and for the most part I am, so I could write his change in attitude as being the result of surviving or maybe even hooking up with me last night…

But something tells me it's not either of those things, and it puts me right the fuck on edge.

He checks his comm tablet, and when I glance at it, my translator manages to spit out a bunch of gobbledygook for the Suevan writing. The map is clear enough, at least, though I can't make heads or tails of any of the script overlaid on the complicated schematics.

"We are approaching the base."

I squint at the open grassland. "There isn't anything out here."

Horatio plops down a few feet away, licking his seven-toed paw with a forked tongue like he doesn't have a care in the world.

Must be nice.

"According to the information the Roth, Nydo, gave us, we should be right on top of it."

"I don't see a base—"

Horatio jumps straight up, hissing and growling in that same horrible high-pitched whine. I immediately clap my hands over my ears. The catlike creature scratches at the ground, all of his hair standing on end.

The air around him shimmers, and I suck in a breath as I realize what we're looking at. At what Horatio discovered.

"It's actively shielding the base. Holy shit," I breathe, dipping my fingers into the illusion.

"Nydo did not tell us of an active illusion energy shield."

"He's a Roth bastard, of course he didn't say shit about it."

"He did not say anything about shit, either. But he was right about the location."

I blink up at him, then shake my head. "We really need to work on your slang. But not right now."

Horatio paws at the forcefield, and it shimmers around his clawed paw. He retracts it, staring at the now invisible energy barrier, then up at me, a plaintive expression on his adorable furry little face.

"It doesn't look like it's charged. Just veiled," I mutter.

"That or the feline has extraordinary pain tolerance."

"One way to find out," I say, sticking my fingers out. No sooner have I brushed the exterior of the forcefield, then something grabs my hand and yanks me through.

"Oh, fuck," I say on an exhale, my heart hammering against my chest. There are deep violet fingers around my wrist. The world rushes around me, the shimmering exterior of the active camouflage rippling across my body. The sun blinks bright, then descends into darkness. I fist my free hand immediately, pulling back to land a punch on whatever—whoever—is holding me.

But another purplish hand stops me before I can.

Blue eyes peer down at me, so dark they're nearly indigo, and I stare up, and *up* at the alien before me.

It's not a Roth.

"Take your hands off my wife," Dergoz growls, a lethal edge to his voice.

The hair on the back of my neck stands up at his tone. It brooks no argument, and the alien newcomer loosens his grip on me immediately. I've been pulled into some kind of dusty shed, and judging from the thick layer of grime coating the machine parts and tools hanging on the walls, it's been unused for a long time.

"I did not know she belonged to you," the alien says.

"She does," Dergoz says, putting a possessive arm around my stomach, drawing me close to him.

He thinks I belong to him. It's ridiculously primal, completely at odds with the fact I've only ever wanted to belong to myself—and the worst part is… I like it.

I like that he sees me as *his*.

"What are *you* doing here?"

I blink at the familiarity with which Dergoz addresses the newcomer. He knows him, I realize.

"We were allies once, Brute. Do not think I have forgotten that. We could be allies again." The alien is one hundred percent male, and even if he *was* wearing clothes, his huge cock would make that glaringly obvious. He's as big as Dergoz, though the blue-black fins on the backs of his arms and legs make him seem even bigger, as do the strange, nearly transparent fins rustling on either side of his face. Glimmering scales iridesce in the bright light, long blue hair falling down his shoulders.

"So uh, I feel like I'm the third wheel here. How do you two know each other?" I ask Dergoz, relaxing a little. If he's not slicing his head off or pulling his spine out, it means he's probably not an enemy. Probably.

"You are not a wheel at all," Dergoz says slowly, casting his gaze around. I follow his stare, landing only on the dim interior of the small, abandoned building we've been pulled into. "I do not see two wheels around us, either. Are you feverish?"

"Nah, I'm just on an idiom roll. Get it? A roll?" I laugh at my own joke, then stop, both aliens staring at me with matching consternated expressions. "It means I'm left out. The odd man out. You two clearly have history, and I have no idea what it is." I shrug, then sigh.

"We fought in the settlement wars together," the alien says. "I am Reif, of the Arco people." He nods his head, his fins fluttering.

The Arco... I blink, trying to place that name. My brain clicks along slowly before landing on a memory. That's right. The marine aliens, the ones that we saw even less of than the Suevans.

Reif eyes me appraisingly, his gaze sliding over my body in blatant appreciation. His lips quirk up in a smile.

"I take it the Roth chatter we picked up is true then, Brute? The human females are compatible breeders? But... why would you bring your stunning human female here?"

In one smooth motion, Dergoz pushes me out of the way, pulling the energy axe from between his shoulders. The blade whines low, and the finned alien swallows, his fins pricking up, a glowing liquid leaking from them.

"Do not get any ideas about my mate. Do not speak of breeding around her. Do not appreciate her beauty. Do not even look at her."

Reif grins at him, raising one eyebrow at me. "I did not mean to offend. And I cannot help looking, Dergoz. It would be rude to pretend she does not exist, would it not?"

Horatio chooses that moment to jump through the door of the shed with an ear-shattering cry. "Yeaaaah!" Every time he says it, I nearly laugh. I had a cat once that sounded like he said hello whenever he meowed, but I never had one that screamed yeah at the top of his lungs.

None of my cats had hundreds of teeth, either.

Reif's eyes go wide. "You brought a divimenton into the Roth base?"

"He's mine," I say. "Don't hurt him."

"As if I could," Reif says with a laugh. "Your human female is full of surprises, Brute. Please, put your weapon down. I do not wish to fight you. I could use your help." His gaze turns crafty. There's more to this Arco than an easy laugh and muscles.

"With what?" Dergoz snarls, clearly still on edge.

I place a hand on his shoulder, trying to calm him down. He shrugs me off, pushing me further behind him. Irritation grows in my gut, as well as a sense of disappointment.

Don't get me wrong, I like when he gets all possessive, but… I'm not a child. I can take care of myself.

"We're here for information about Roth plans about Earth," I say frankly, peering around Dergoz's stupidly broad torso. It's probably a lot less smooth than something Michelle might say, and God only knows what Niki would say about me blurting our mission here, but it is what it is.

"I am here for my brother. If you help me retrieve him, I will help you with your information gathering." He says the last two words with thick amusement, and I have the strong impression Reif thinks our mission is stupid.

"Why is your brother here? Our intelligence only said that this base was used for data storage and as a small launch point into neutral territory."

"Then your intelligence is old, my friend."

"What do you mean?" I ask slowly, ignoring Dergoz's growl of irritation at being called Reif's friend.

"This is not simply some data center. This is their forward operating base, giving them another foothold into enemy territory." The words are said with a guttural snarl completely at odds with the massive alien's previously easy-going demeanor. "Into Arco territory. They mean to subsume our planet, just as they tried to with the settlements, when we rained death on them."

His fins are standing at full attention, the blue seeping away, replaced by a deep crimson, the color of blood.

Dergoz stands a little straighter, his tail flicking into my leg, before stroking against my pant leg reassuringly. "I will help you find your brother, Reif."

The Arco glances at me, his lips pursed in contemplation. "And your wife? What will you do, little human?"

The shed is suddenly too small, thick with tension between the two alien warriors. If I had a butter knife, I'm pretty sure it wouldn't cut it. I'd need a butcher knife to get through it. I'm half-surprised I'm not straight up choking on all the alien testosterone the two are emitting.

"I'm in," I say easily.

"No," Dergoz snarls, and it takes me a moment to realize what he's saying.

Horatio rubs his whiskered cheek against my knee, sitting at my feet like a trained dog. Cat. Lion-cheetah-cat-dog. Divimenton.

"What do you mean, 'no?'" I ask, narrowing my eyes and poking at Dergoz's thickly muscled shoulder. "What do you plan to have me do?"

"This place seems as safe as any," Dergoz says slowly, turning to give me a quelling look over one shoulder. "You can stay here."

"Like hell I'm going to stay here!" I whisper-shout, remembering at the last minute to keep my voice down.

"He simply wishes to keep the mother of his future brood safe," Reif interjects.

"Shut up," Dergoz and I snap at him at the same time.

Reif shrugs. "Just trying to—"

"I am not staying here while you two go off and save the day. Nope. Fuck that. I am coming with you. You need me. You admitted it yourself!"

"No, my feisty little human, I *needed* you. Now I have Reif."

Aghast, I look between them, completely annoyed and feeling… hurt. Which is exactly why it doesn't pay to grow feelings for the alien you're trying to fuck. Man. Whatever. They all end up hurting your feelings when you get invested.

"He is just trying to protect you, delicate human female."

I crook a finger at the finned alien. Horatio yowls in response, and Reif's eyes widen slightly. "If I wanted your opinion, you overgrown fish-man, then I'd ask for it. Shut it."

"She is quite fierce for such a soft creature—"

"Shut the fuck up!" I yell at him. Horatio screams again, and Reif takes a step back. I advance on Dergoz, utterly annoyed and completely furious. "You don't get to leave me behind, Dergoz. I'm not going to sit on my ass here and wait to be found by the Roth."

"Then come along," he says easily.

I narrow my eyes, tilting my head as I inspect him.

"We will steal you a ship and put you spaceside at the first opportunity," he finishes.

Reif groans, and I throw my hands into the air.

"And there it is!" I say. Reif nods sympathetically until I shoot him a killing glance. "I might not be scaly, or finned, or eight feet tall, but I am good with a gun and I am great with tech. I am a military officer. I am trained. And I am capable. I will not let you sideline me just because you want to shove a kid inside me." That didn't come out quite right, but I'm too mad to correct myself.

"That is not how you become pregnant," Dergoz says easily. "The baby grows inside of you. I do not force the baby into your body."

I walk over to the wall and slam my forehead against it twice before leaning against it completely. Sure, I'm covered in dust now, but I was already filthy, so whatever.

"Your mate does not seem pleased with your directive," Reif says.

The fish alien really does not know when to keep his gob shut.

"I do not wish you to become injured," Dergoz says quietly. "Do not hit your head on the metal again or I will be forced to take drastic measures."

Agog, I glance over my shoulder at him. "What the fuck is that supposed to mean?"

"I will tie you up and leave you here."

"You would not."

"I would do anything to keep you safe, and you are demonstrating right now that I cannot trust you to take care of yourself."

"Are you fucking kidding me? I would not mind being tied up in bed, but I swear to God, Dergoz, if you tie me up to keep me safe right now, I will never forgive you. Can't you see that would put me in more danger."

"I did not know humans enjoyed binding games," Reif says thoughtfully, his eyes glittering with arousal.

"Now's not the time, Reif!" I bark at him. Horatio yowls in agreement. "At this rate, it's amazing we haven't triggered any alarms with as much noise as we've been making."

"I have a silencer on this foul place. No one can hear anything."

Dergoz steps toward me, a manic gleam in his eye.

"Don't you fucking dare," I spit at him, desperation and fear starting to claw at me. "Don't you dare tie me up and leave me here."

"I only want to keep you safe."

"I feel this is a poor decision," Reif says, looking between us with a faintly concerned furrow to his scaly blue-purple brow.

"As far as I recall, no one has asked for your opinion," Dergoz snarls.

"I don't know, I think you should listen to him," I say blithely. Dergoz takes another step toward me, and this time, I don't want him to come any closer.

I shrink into the wall, looking for a way to escape. But the huge alien male advances steadily, and for the first time, I'm truly aware of the power differential between us.

"Don't do this," I tell him. "Don't you fucking dare."

"I would move planets if I thought it would keep you safe. I would move the very stars themselves if I thought it gave me a chance to make things right between us."

"This will only make things wrong between us," I say, snarling, my fingers curled into fists at my side.

I don't get a chance to move though, because the Brute is on me before I even get a chance to throw a punch.

I'm too mad to even speak as he winds a length of rope around my wrists and ankles.

There is a look of faint regret and unease on his face, though that does absolutely nothing to melt my fury. In fact, it might just make it worse, considering he clearly knows he's being an asshat.

"You're an asshat," I tell him, struggling against the bindings.

"You will be perfectly safe," Dergoz tells me, as though I haven't spoken at all.

"That is not entirely true," Reif says, his mouth curled to one side. "I can leave the silencer up, though."

"Horatio will guard you. He is a formidable opponent."

"Do not fucking leave me!" I yell.

"Here," he says, handing his comms tablet to Reif. "I assume you can add your tablet, so that she may contact us if necessary?"

"This seems ill-advised, my friend," Reif says, shaking his head. "Nevertheless, I will do as you wish."

Dergoz's eyes are full of that manic light, his entire body bristling with an electric tension that screams his discomfort.

I shimmy against the bonds, trying to loosen them somewhat, but they're tight as hell.

"Normally, this might be a turn-on," I say angrily, "but right now? Right now I want to punch you right in your handsome face."

"I will remember your preferences for our marital bed," Dergoz replies.

"You bastard. I don't want to be in your marital bed now! You are betraying me. You lied to me and tied me up!"

"You will get over it, because you will be safe. You can thank me later."

Reif's long fingers glide over the tablet surface, and holographic images float around his hand as he manipulates the screen.

I squint at it. It doesn't look like he's just linking his tablet to it. I don't have time to decipher what, exactly, he's doing though, because Dergoz crouches before me, his mouth pressing against mine.

Heat swells within me at the contact, my body reacting even though I'm furious with him. Too late, I turn my head away, my lips pursed.

Dergoz stays there though, a hair's breadth away from my lips, his warm breath washing over my face. "You will forgive me in time," he says, a note of triumph in his voice. As though he knows exactly how my body's responded, in spite of my pulling away from him.

And with his stupid nose, he probably does know.

It makes me madder, and I struggle against the rope cinching my wrists.

"You're wrong," I tell him, absolutely livid. "I will remember this forever."

He blinks at the force of my words, and Reif awkwardly looks between us.

"Then we best hurry, Dergoz, so that your fierce mate has every opportunity to forgive you more quickly."

Dergoz stands quickly, and as he turns toward the door, Reif throws a wink at me, the expression so human, so at odds with everything about him, that it catches me completely off guard. I stop struggling, staring up at him warily.

Dergoz casts me one last apologetic look before leaving in Reif's wake.

Horatio settles in my lap, the comms tablet on the dirty ground beside me. He purrs contentedly, little seven-toed paws kneading the ground in front of me.

"I do not think you made the right choice for your mate," Reif's voice says, and I glance up, expecting to see him in the doorway.

But he's not there. Neither of them are there.

The voice is coming from the comms tablet, clear as day. Horatio shares a startled glance up at me, then returns to kneading the ground, sharp claws leaving deep punctures.

Reif made it to where he's transmitting live to the comms tablet at my side. I can, at the very least, listen in.

"I really wish you could get me out of here." Too bad Horatio can't untie my stupid ropes, much less understand me. I grit my teeth. I'm so angry I can hardly see straight, hardly think straight.

How dare he truss me up and leave me in Roth territory? I thought we'd come to an understanding. I thought we were on the same page; hell, I thought he respected me.

Well he respects me enough for sex, but not enough to trust me to come along on this mission and be anything but a liability. Of all the heavy-handed, asshole things to do.

Horatio blinks owlishly at me, then moseys off my lap, rubbing his face against my arms and wrists as he prowls behind me.

A moment later, I feel a raspy tongue lick my forearms.

"I really hope Dergoz didn't know shit when he said you were poisonous," I mutter.

Something sharp nicks my wrists, and I flinch before I realize what's happening.

Horatio is chewing through the ties around my wrists.

DERGOZ

GUILT GNAWS AT ME.

"I did the right thing," I grumble, but Reif just shoots me a frown before jerking his head towards the hatch in the ground.

"I could not stand to see her hurt." Surely she will understand that I acted out of care, out of concern. That I acted out of… love.

Still. I feel… ashamed. That I left her there, when she has proven she is capable.

I cannot stand to see her hurt on my mission.

Or for her to see what I truly am. A monster.

And with the knowledge that this is a forward operating base of the Roth, there is no doubt in my mind that I will have to be the Brute yet again, as distasteful as the idea is.

The sun beats down on my scales, warmth spreading along them as we make our way to the door that will lead to the underground operations base. According to Nydo's intel, the base opens up to a cliffside, which allows for aircraft to come and go more stealthily, but makes for a single entrance and thus makes it harder for the base to be infiltrated, especially with the live camouflage barrier.

So far, we have met with no resistance, which is raising all kinds of internal alarm bells.

"This is likely a trap," I tell Reif as he reaches for the lever that will open the hatch.

"That makes it all the more fun, don't you agree?"

I grunt. "Then it was a good idea I left my mate in the house, yes?"

"Oh, no," Reif says cheerily. "That was sheer idiocy. The woman could be useful. I do not know much about their species, other than they successfully repelled a Roth invasion once, despite being severely underpowered. I do know that a mate should be an equal partner, however and you are definitely fucking that up quite well."

"What do you know of mates?"

"I know enough to know that I would seek all the dark sides of every planet to find mine, and here you are, tying yours up and leaving her alone in a filthy hovel against her will."

"You should not sound so pleased about it."

"Why wouldn't I be? Perhaps the creature will decide to leave with me if you continue to treat her so poorly."

I growl at him, my glare promising death. "Find your own human."

"Oh, I very much intend to, now that I have met one face-to-face. Though I would much prefer meeting her body-to-body."

I round on him, fury rising in me. "She is mine. I wed her in a time-honored Suevan ceremony."

"She did not bear your mated scent," Reif says casually, as if he does not care that I am a moment away from slicing his face off. Or ripping his spine off. Perhaps I will do both.

"There is no reason to look murderous, old friend."

"I am not your friend, and the human female is mine."

"Then why is she tied up in a shed when she repeatedly told you not to do that? Kidnapping a mate is a beloved Arco tradition, but I do not think your female would like that."

A harsh noise spills out of me, and I pace beside the hatch. He might be right.

She will be safer there.

I cannot bear to see the terror on her face again. I cannot bear to see her hurt. Better she be mad at me for all her remaining years than to have them cut short by a Roth weapon.

The hatch opens quietly, without a sound, as though the door is kept well-maintained, despite the above-ground ghost town.

"It is oddly quiet," Reif muses. "Would you like to go first?"

"I will go first if you are too big of a coward to," I snarl.

"Well, I was not the one who was too afraid to bring my mate along for fear of her being hurt, or fear that I could not keep her well protected," Reif says with a shrug, his back fins fluttering.

"Shut your mouth when you talk about my mate."

He grimaces at me, turning to descend into the darkness below. "That does not make any sense, Brute. It seems your brain has stopped working for the need to rut the soft female."

I cannot even bring myself to respond. I am too furious with Reif's empty threats to steal my Ree-becca away. My Bex, my funny, smart, and beautiful human.

Who is safer tied up in the abandoned shed than she would be on this mission at my side. And if she hates me afterwards, at least it is for protecting her, and not for seeing how truly monstrous I can be.

"Perhaps I will have to find a shipment of these human females for myself… and for my own men. Put them in one of the houses of Arco and keep them there until they succumb to our advances."

"They are not goods to be shipped about and held against their will." I step foot on the ladder. "They are brilliant strategists, quick-witted and funny. They are good in a tight spot, and they have feelings, just as we all do."

"Ah. So you would advise against locking one up when she does not want to be?"

"Of course, I would," I spit, closing the hatch door overhead, causing low lights to flicker on in the tunnel. It's a tight enough space that I need to tuck my tail close into my body, my shoulders brushing against the sides. Reif's fins are likewise tucked in tight to his body below me.

He makes an amused noise. "I find it very interesting that you would deign to give me such advice, when you yourself have locked your own mate up, tied her up so she cannot defend herself, and left her with a divimenton as her only protection."

"She has the comms tablet in case she needs to call for help."

"Indeed, she does. I can only hope she is able to utilize it quickly enough, were the worst case scenario to happen."

"She is safer there!" I snarl, climbing down, down, down, my voice echoing off the metallic chamber.

"Very well." He sighs, but I know from experience, the Arco is far from done talking about how I've left Bex. "Truly though, do you think the Earth Federation would be amenable to sending more women to my planet?"

"The virus has ravaged your world as well?" I shake my head. "I am sorry to hear that."

"We were able to stop it, mostly, by quarantining as many of our young females as possible. It tore through all the females of mating age, though." His voice is weary, and I feel a surge of sympathy for the huge, finned alien. "My men and I… we were certain that we would swim alone for the rest of our lives."

"The Earth females are not aquatic. They cannot breathe underwater. I am not sure they would be able to survive on your planet."

"You do not know much of Arco." There's a hint of a smile to his voice, despite the terrible news.

"Do you think we walk into a trap?" I change the subject, sniffing the air. It has the metallic quality of recycled life support systems, and the much stronger scent of Roth.

"I think we likely descend into one, not so much walk," he answers. I roll my eyes. Everyone thinks they're a comedian.

"How was your brother captured?" It is no easy feat to take an

Arco. They are fearsome warriors, and until we brokered a peace with them on the distant settlements, we were concerned that they would pose a real threat in battle.

They do; just not to the Suevans. Not anymore.

"There was talk of a female," Reif says. His voice is weary, the light humor that colors his usual tone gone. "That one of mating age was taken from the settlements by the Roth. It was a female he knew from our homeworld."

"They lied," I finish.

"The female is long dead. But he came anyway, hoping for her to be here. It was a ruse, and now they use my brother's captivity as leverage to try to gain a foothold in Arco."

"Fucking Roth," I snarl.

"The Overlord is a twisted one," he says. "If only the true leader of their people would return."

I frown. I've heard whispers about a ruler in hiding, but I thought them just that: foundless rumors from a species in dire need for hope.

"Finally," Reif says, and soon enough, my own feet reach solid ground.

We're in their underground bunker.

"First, we find the intel on their Earth and Sueva missions."

"And Arco," Reif says, his voice taking on a low rasp that speaks of violence.

"And then we find your brother."

"Agreed."

He touches his side, and a long sword appears, its camouflage tech deactivating as he swings it in front of him, where it blazes like a star in the dark underground base.

"That thing is going to draw more attention than we'd like."

"If this is a trap," he answers, "and I am sure that it is, then at least the Roth will know who killed them before I gut them like an Arcon fish."

"Not if I debone them first," I say, cracking my knuckles.

He chuckles, but there isn't any humor in the sound. "I didn't know you had it in you to make a joke."

I start to tell him that perhaps my smart, funny mate has rubbed off on me, but then I remember how she told me she would never forget me leaving her bound in that shed, and I swallow the words.

Maybe I should have brought her along, after all.

It's too late now.

Besides, she's safer there, anyway.

BEX

"THIS CAN'T BE SAFE. This is not good." It's the fourth or fifth time I've said this. Listening to the two scaled idiots bicker about fucking me on the comms tablet didn't improve my mood, strangely enough.

Normally, I'd be all for an alien *why choose* scenario, but real life, it turns out, does differ from fiction.

Because I want only *one* of them.

Even though I am absolutely livid with the big green beanstalk of a lizardman.

"I'm so mad, Horatio," I say. The cat still gnaws at the cords tying my wrists together. I jiggle my leg, sending up a puff of dust from the floor.

"Yeaaaaaaaah," Horatio yowls in agreement. At least, it sounds like that. I don't think he's actually agreeing with me, though he certainly seemed to correctly interpret my desire to get the fuck out of this abandoned shed. And walk right into what they both suspect is a Roth trap!

What a pair of fluff for brains.

"My blood is literally boiling," I tell the cat, who keeps chewing. "Not really literally, though. Figuratively doesn't have quite the same ring to it, you know? Either way, I'm pissed. How could he? He legit left me here like a sitting duck, tied up for whatever Roth fuckface decides to come by and do whatever with me."

The thought sends my heart hammering against my chest, and anger spikes all over again.

Dergoz and Reif have gone quiet on the comms tablet, and the only sound Reif's transmitting is the echo of their footfalls in the underground bunker. I'm grateful for that. At least the bunker isn't cutting off their comms completely, something I was worried about.

Of course, there's no guarantee that will continue the deeper they go into the base.

I need to get down there with them, and I need to do it fast. Because the further they descend, the less likely it is that I'll be able to hear if they need help.

And based on their deductions that they're walking into a trap, they're going to sure as shit need me.

"What were they thinking?" I ask Horatio, who mewls at me. "Completely ruled by one brain cell and their dicks."

I kick my foot, which accomplishes exactly nothing, but makes me feel marginally better.

Suddenly, my wrists are free, and I wince as I pull them around, rubbing off the sting from where the ropes were.

I squint at the rope burn, and it's worse than I would expect… blistered and red. Poking at it, I let out a small hiss as pain spikes through me.

Horatio lets out a plaintive mewl.

"Thanks, you little biblical angel," I tell him, scratching him under his chin. "You did really good." My hand stops when I catch sight of the remainder of the cord Dergoz used to tie me.

It's not just chewed through. It's partially melted.

Horatio mews again.

"Fuck," I say, my eyes huge. "You *are* poisonous, aren't you?

Don't tell Dergoz that. We'll keep it a little secret between us." I throw my head back. "Ugh! I'm so mad!"

Honestly, the women on my crew went out of their way to keep me happy.

It's not hard, either. I'm not quick to anger. I like to be happy. I like low drama. Well, I like a little drama, but only the low-stakes fun kind. Not the being tied up, left for dead at a Roth forward operating base kind.

No, they liked to keep me happy because I am hell on wheels when I'm pissed. Yeah, it takes me a while to get there, but when I am? All bets are off.

And whooooooo, buddy, am I there now.

"I'm fucking mad," I say again, stretching out and standing up. Horatio wraps around my legs in a figure eight, his tails fanning out behind him as he waits for me to take the lead on whatever adventure we're about to have. "Thanks for staying with me and melting the ropes off, you terrible little alien companion, my sweet bugaboo baby-face kitten-head," I tell him in my best baby voice, earning a deep purr. "Who's ready to go kill some Roths, huh? Who's gonna bitey-bite their faces off? Who's going to acid melt their stupid gray skin, huh? I bet you are! I bet you are!!!"

Horatio lets out another yowl, which sounds exactly like a long, angry, '*Yeaaaaaaah!*'

Frankly, it raises all the hair on the back of my neck.

I'm glad Horatio is on my side.

The comms tablet makes a noise from where it lays on the ground, and I pick it up, listening intently. Horatio sits on top of my feet, his tails flicking against my leg.

There's no mistaking the sound emitting from the tablet.

That's plasma fire.

And neither Reif nor Dergoz carried a plasma rifle with them.

"In the words of the great Britney Spears," I tell the cat, "you better work, bitch."

He rubs his head against my boot in agreement. Well, maybe not agreement, exactly, but it does kind of seem like he's nodding.

A little anthropomorphism never hurt anybody!

Well, except all the random people keeping tigers as pets who then were surprised when the tigers tried to eat their faces.

I cast a sidelong look at Horatio, who stares up at me, his tails slashing back and forth behind him.

"You wouldn't eat my face, would you?"

He blinks at me.

"I'm going to take that as a no." I squint at him, like he's going to change his mind and suddenly start eating my face.

"Fuck," Dergoz's voice slices through the air, and the sound of plas pulse fire intensifies.

"This is worse than we thought," Reif says, grunting.

"That's what they get, those selfish fucks," I tell Horatio. "Well, do you think we should roll in and save the day, or what?"

He blinks twice at me.

"And I'm going to call that a yes. You know, I'm pretty sure my grandparents used to watch a show where the horse used his hoof to talk."

Horatio hisses at me, as though the mere thought of a talking horse is enough to set his teeth, all eleventy-billion of them, on edge.

"I have been hit," Dergoz grunts. "Flee, Reif. Save yourself."

The hair stands on the back of my neck, chills descending all along my bare arms. "Shit," I whisper.

A huge boom echoes through the comm, and the ground shakes. Horatio makes an incredible vertical jump, his tails fluffing out completely, all his fur standing on end. I brace myself against the walls.

That was a plas grenade. For sure. I witnessed enough of them fighting against the Roth to know a plas grenade when I feel one. And Dergoz is hurt.

My chest aches. As mad, nah, furious, as I am with him, I don't want him to be hurt. I can't stand the thought of it. Him lying in the underground base, bleeding, without me.

Anger burns through me. He should have brought me with them!

"I will not leave you here," Reif says, his voice coming in between deep pants.

"You are bleeding," Dergoz says, "but you can still make it. Leave me, Reif. Take care of my Ree-becca. See her safely back to Sueva."

"I will not leave you," Reif says, ice in his words.

Another boom sounds, and the floor quakes again, Horatio hissing at it.

"You tell 'em," I say, but my voice is hollow and devoid of humor.

I stare at the comms tablet, rifling through options. No way in hell am I prancing into a Roth base in my underwear and singing my way into helping those two scaled knuckleheads. I need a real plan this time. Not some half-cocked idea about getting every-one's cocks at half-mast.

Fuck. I wish Niki or Gen were here, or Michelle.

My breath's coming too fast, the sounds of the firefight below my feet still trickling through the comms tablet.

It's over quickly though, the Roth rattling off commands to take them to the rest of the prisoners as I listen in horror.

"I thought one was a female," one of the Roth says, his voice coming crisp over the comm link.

"Only the two of us, I'm afraid," Reif says, and his casual humor's firmly in place. "No females here. If you'd like to check, though—" his voice dies in a grunt of pain.

"Your brother is not nearly as funny as you are," a Roth voice says, dripping with sarcasm. "But he is a much better screamer."

"You fucker—" the comm link dies, cutting off whatever Reif was about to say.

Oh my God. I scrub a hand down my face, trying to think.

Trying to focus past the fear gripping me, fear for Dergoz and now for Reif and his brother too.

I glance around the small space, trying to take stock of what I have.

There's an alien tool that looks somewhat like a weed whacker. Maybe I could use that.

A vision pops into my head, of me screaming obscenities as I plow down the Roth with a weed whacker. Okay. Better than nothing.

I have Horatio. He's a badass. I don't want him to get hurt though, either, and plas pulse rifles and plas grenades are very, very different from a herd of alien antelopes. Still, Horatio is coming with me.

I clutch the comm tablet to my chest, trying to find something, anything else, that I could take into my impromptu and ill-advised rescue mission.

The scrambler. I need to find the noise silencer and maybe figure out how to reverse engineer it so it can shield me. It won't work like camouflage or hide my heat signature, but it might be enough to throw them off, and I'll take anything I can get.

My fingers scrape down the sides of the comm tablet, and I pet it, getting solace from the familiar tech.

That's it! I have my brain, too. If I can find their awful computer and hack into it, I can have these fuckers at my mercy. There is no one better than me at causing mayhem in a computer system. That's what my college professor always said, anyways.

The comm tablet vibrates in my hand as a message comes in, showing that the connection to Reif has been officially lost.

Oh, biscuits and gravy, but I'm an idiot.

I have the comm tablet.

My fingers fly over the screen, holographic projections sliding across my skin as I find my way into the classified comms system that will link me back to Sueva.

Fuck. I can't read the Suevan symbols, so I just pick the first name on the list and hope for the best.

After a few rings, Draz's face fills the space between me and the tablet, and I nearly faint in relief.

"Thank fuck it's you. Listen, this mission has gone tits up."

"Where the hell have you been?" Niki's voice sears through the comm link. "We have been worried sick about you."

"There's not time for that shit right now," I snarl, sounding a little too like Dergoz for my own liking. "We need a rescue. My cranky asshole of a husband has been captured by the Roth, along with a fish merman alien named Reif." My forehead wrinkles as it hits me. "Frankly, his name's a little too on the nose, if you ask me. Anyway, everything's fucked. Dergoz has been shot. We need a rescue and an evac."

"He knew the cost of going to the base."

"Fuck that shit, Draz."

The huge First Warlord glowers at me, and I stick my tongue out at him. "I don't fucking care. You either help me rescue him, or I make my way back to Sueva and make your life a living hell."

"She'll do it, too," Niki says, but there's no humor in her expression. "What do you need, Bex?"

"I want the Roth. I want the Roth, and I want whoever you can spare for backup."

"You want us to release Nydo… for a rescue mission… against the Roth," Draz repeats slowly. "To say this is poorly thought out barely scrapes the surface of how terrible a—"

"This plan is pig-fucked," Niki cuts him off. "What are you thinking?"

So I tell her exactly what I'm thinking, and by the time I'm done, Draz is nodding his head, a thoughtful, calculating light in his diamond-pupiled eyes.

"Do you think I can trust him?" I finally ask. It seems like too much time has passed. I want to hurry, but I need to do this right.

"He is different from the other Roth I have had the misfortune of dealing with."

"It's a risk," Niki adds, her brow furrowed, in full captain mode. We used to joke that when she'd get like this, she'd need a whole barrel of candy to calm down after.

"Do you think it's worth it?"

"I do," she says.

Draz nods his head slowly in agreement. "I think he has a secret. But I also think he hates the Overlord and what he's done more than we do."

"Will he go for it?"

"Only one way to find out. But the soonest anyone can be planet side and where you are is at least a full day away."

"You won't need to come in stealthily. Come in hot, make it look good."

"And will you wait for him there?" Niki's eyes narrow, and we both already know the answer to that question.

"No. Dergoz might be a grumpy piece of shit, but he's my grumpy piece of shit. And if anyone is going to make him pay for leaving me here, it's going to be me, and not the Roth." I'm already thinking up new ways that he can make it up to me, once I make him admit he was wrong. Several times, I think.

"So you're just going to waltz in there and get captured yourself?"

"Maybe," I say.

Niki grimaces, sharing a glance with Draz, who taps out a message on a separate comms pad. "Maybe I don't want to know."

"Could be," I agree. Horatio screams, and I sigh. "Get them here as fast as you can."

"Working on it already. Stay alive."

"Do not let Dergoz die, either, female human," Draz orders me.

"That's the plan, Stan."

"Who is Stan?" Draz frowns, and Niki pats his arm.

"Let it go," she says. "Come on. We have work to do. Be careful, Bex."

"I always am."

"No, you're not, but I bet that's why you're going to make it out alive."

"Because I'm one crazy son of a bitch."

Niki grins at me. "Something like that."

"She is… calling her mother a bitch?" Draz asks her, his fingers paused over his tablet.

"Good luck, Officer Abbas."

"Thank you, Captain Jacks." Her title rolls off my tongue, as sure as it did the first time we crewed together a few years ago. It sounds strange now, foreign, almost. "Warlord Niki."

Her smile deepens, and then the comms tablet goes dark.

I tilt my head back, blowing out a breath and studying the metal ceiling.

It's time to get to work.

CHAPTER
TWENTY-TWO

DERGOZ

MY SIDE ACHES. My head aches. Blood leaks from the wound in my shoulder. It's deep enough to hurt, but not deep enough to do more than that. Though the amount of blood I'm losing is alarming, it's not cause for concern.

Being taken deeper into the Roth base, however, is a slightly different matter.

Reif moves slowly behind me, one of his delicate spiked fins ripped where it meets his leg. The Roth soldiers secured us with manacles and chains, and there is no hope of escape.

All I could think of when they clapped the metal onto my scales was that I had done the same to my Bex.

I will go to my death grateful that she is alive and regretting that I caused her so much pain during our short, ill-fated marriage. And hating that I was too stubborn to seek her out immediately, to set things right between us.

The lights grow brighter the further into the base we descend, and my ears pop more than once as they take us lower and lower. Finally, we reach their prison cells. A motley assortment of mostly female alien species huddle in the corners of their cells, and while there are an assortment of wounds on each of them, no one appears starving or even dirty, as I would expect of a Roth prison.

I sniff the air hesitantly, expecting a foul odor to singe my nostrils, but it smells like antiseptic and soap.

It smells as though the prisoners are cared for.

My tail flicks back and forth.

Reif growls a warning as it slaps against his ankle.

"Apologies," I murmur.

"No talking." The remark is punctuated with a firm rap across my wounded shoulder. Enough that pain lances through me, but not enough to truly bring me to my knees.

Curious. The Roth are typically derive pleasure from inflicting pain, going over the top in their cruelty towards their enemies.

But this prison, these holding cells... They are well lit. The prisoners seem well taken care of. Where we would have been mistreated as prisoners of war during the settlement battles, they are handling us with a soft touch that raises all kinds of internal alarms.

Reif glances over at me, and I wonder if he's thinking the same thing: that they've either changed how they operate, or they're saving the worst for later, lulling us into false complacency, a false sense of security.

A plastitech door hisses open, and a guard shoves me inside. I pace the back of the cell, their plasma weapons trained on me, as Reif is thrown into an adjacent cell across the corridor. A light flickers on in a cell directly opposite mine, revealing the half-asleep but stirring occupants.

Shock courses through me, and I barely stop myself from approaching the plastitech door and no doubt earning another plasma pulse.

The cell is full of humans.

Human women. And not just any human females, but judging from their tattered uniforms, Federation officers. Just like my Reebecca.

They blink at me, weariness and wariness etched across their young, delicate faces.

Worry slides through me, insidious, churning through my stomach and leaving me cold. Will they find Bex? Will she join these women in this prison?

What the fuck are the Roth up to?

What have I done?

Have I saved Bex by leaving her behind, or have I condemned her to a horrible fate at the hand of these Roths?

CHAPTER
TWENTY-THREE

BEX

I SHOULDN'T RUSH into this. "I shouldn't hurry it," I tell Horatio, pacing back and forth. I didn't realize it when they abandoned me here, but Dergoz left a small pack of food and the water canteen, and I'm chewing the supplements furiously as my feet make a furrow in the dirt floor.

The silencer is half taken apart on a workbench, and I work on it as I chew, trying to rewire it to work more as a personal stealth machine than a massive area effect.

The Arco tech isn't too far off from the Suevan's, and I'm super glad I spent so much time fiddling with stuff in their labs for the last few weeks.

I don't want to run in without a plan.

I don't think I can afford to wait on the rescue back-up Niki and Draz have promised, but I know I shouldn't go tearing into the hatch without something more well thought out than, 'hey, this is probably a trap, but I'm big and green and a badass people call the Brute.'

Unfortunately, all my plans seem to run the same risk of being captured as theirs did. I really don't want to get shot, though. I don't have the benefit of a massively bullet resistant exterior like the two alien clowns that now need a rescue from yours truly.

I snort a laugh at the mental image of Dergoz and Reif in clown paint, then squeeze my eyes shut, trying to refocus my hyperactive brain.

Now is not the time for that!

Horatio sneezes in his sleep, and I jump, startled at the sudden noise.

My plan for the rescuers is clear in my head, and Niki and Draz seemed to think it would work.

At least if I get caught, rescue will be hot on my heels.

I narrow my eyes.

Is my plan to get caught? Could there be a worse plan?

If my time with Dergoz and the Roth have taught me anything, it's that they both underestimate me at their own peril. I've never liked being underestimated, but maybe... maybe this time I can use that to my advantage.

An evil grin turns up the corners of my lips. I wish I had a goatee for occasions like this, just so I could twist it around my finger and cackle maniacally. Really complete the image.

I settle for a small unhinged giggle, causing Horatio to open one baleful eye.

"I am going to get caught and it is going to be an absolute party," I tell him. "I hope you're ready." My mouth twists to the side. "Wait, I don't want them to hurt you."

Huh. How am I supposed to sneak my nightmare kitty into their base? If I look sideways at him, it's almost like he's grown by the hour.

"Babies," I sigh. "You grow up so fast."

"Yeaaaaaaaah!" Horatio yells in agreement.

"Okay, so if I tell you to stay here, will you listen?"

He blinks at me.

"Was one blink no or yes? I can't remember the system." It's official, I've lost my marbles. Not sure the marbles I had left were quality, but man, am I going to miss them. I crack my knuckles, stretching my neck out.

"Just a few more adjustments," I mutter. My fingers shake slightly as I reconnect several of the tiny chips in the complex tech, adjusting several others with a tiny nudge. "That should do it."

Only one way to find out.

I place the hard shell back on top of the silencer, sending up a silent plea that this will work, that I can get inside the main frame and get us all out safely. Or, at the very least, wreak enough havoc that it makes it easier on our rescue and evac team.

As soon as I swipe the panel to activate the silencer, an ear-splitting noise screams from the machine.

"Alright then," I say, adrenaline spiking. "Not exactly what I had in mind, but that will do, I guess."

I slip several of the components I pulled out into my bra, along with some parts I scrapped from the shed. Sure, my boobs look bulkier than normal, and if anyone touches them, they'll wonder why they're hard as hell, but beggars can't be choosers!

Maybe I can just play it off as an alien thing.

Ah yes, sir Roth, this is what human boobs look like! Lumpy and hard. Very normal. These are not the boobs you're looking for.

I sit down heavily, winding the mostly frayed rope around my wrists and motioning for Horatio to sit with me. They won't shoot him. When in doubt, cry it out.

Time to play off my husband's worst nightmare.

Heh. The look on his face when he sees I've been captured? Payback's a bitch!

I've started to grow bored by the time the first Roth appears. The plas rifle appears first, then the Roth edges in, his eyes widening upon finding me tied up on the floor.

"Finally," I murmur. "Oh thank the HEAVENS," I screech at him. "That beast, that Suevan monster, he tied me up and left me here! Thank GOD you're here to save me from him."

My chest heaves, and I wail, only to have Horatio join me. I cut him a look, the spotlight thief, and he snaps his mouth shut, blinking slowly.

The Roth stares at us, open-mouthed.

"Please, please say you'll help me." A solitary tear tracks down my cheek, my tear ducts betraying me. Fake crying's never been a real tool in my arsenal, but the Roth appears agitated at the liquid.

A second Roth appears, likewise flummoxed by the sight of me on the floor, the silencer screaming, the alien nightmare kitty curled up by my hip.

Can't say I blame him.

"What is she doing out here? Did she escape from the rest of them?"

My ears perk up, and I stop fake crying momentarily. The rest of them? What the fuck does that mean?

"It's a different one, can't you tell? This one has black hair. And her uniform is different."

"All the human females look the same."

"They do not," the first Roth says, aghast. "Are your eyes malfunctioning?"

Shit. They have more humans here? This isn't part of the plan. But I guess it could be!

Thinking on my feet, that's me. Or my ass, as the case may be.

"They are not Roth," the one sniffs, staring at me. "They are not our people."

"You and I both know we are beyond that," the first Roth snaps. "Come on little human, we will take you to your people."

Shit. Why are they being nice? I was prepared for outright warfare. I don't really know what to do with nice. And I don't want them to put me with humans. I mean, I would make it work, but I know who I want to get stuck with. I need to get stuck with him.

"Oh please, please, that would be wonderful." I sniffle a little, and the Roth stares at me in a mixture of curiosity and disgust. What, they don't get boogers? Seems unlikely.

"She has something leaking from her eyes. Is she ill?"

"No, all the humans do that. It must be a species-wide problem."

"There isn't room for more human females in their holding cell."

I watch them warily. "I can't leave my cat behind, he has to come with me."

Horatio hisses at them.

"See? He's friendly," I say.

"That does not seem like a friendly sound."

The second Roth sidesteps us, turning off the screaming silencer, and blessed quiet fills the shack.

"He's protective of me." A lightbulb goes off in my head, and I blurt the words before it decides to spontaneously combust. "The only one he responds to is the huge Suevan Warlord who trapped me here." I blink rapidly, managing to squeeze another tear out. Eat your heart out, Hollywood! "It's probably only safe if you put us with him."

The Roth exchange a look. "I thought you said he was a monster," one says.

Right. "HE IS," I wail, and Horatio takes up the cry, screaming YEAAAAAAAH at the sound of my fake distress.

Both Roth wince.

"But I wouldn't want anyone else to get hurt because of me or my cat, and I am willing to put my selfishness on hold to ensure that everyone is safe," I struggle to my feet, or pretend to, holding the ropes tight in my fists. "I can't have any more murders on my conscious."

"Any more?"

"The Brute is dangerous," I whisper conspiratorially. "But I can handle him."

"Is that who the Suevan is?" the Roth asks, looking nervous for the first time. "The Brute? And you feel safe around him?"

I blink, slightly flustered by their obvious fear. "Why shouldn't I? I mean, no. Of course not. But why?"

"Because he's known for tearing off legs and arms and beating his opponents to death with them."

"Or feeding them their own appendages and organs." The second Roth shudders.

Can't say I was expecting to hear that. "Oh, that old chestnut?"

"What is a chestnut?"

"If she speaks the truth and is that monster's mate, then perhaps we can use her as leverage."

My nose wrinkles. I don't *love* the sound of that.

"He will be furious if you hurt me."

"We aren't going to hurt you," the first Roth laughs. "We need you."

I glance between them, trying to suss out exactly what is going on. None of this is going how I planned it to. I mean, they're taking me to the bunker, they haven't beat the shit out of me, and they've agreed to get me and Horatio to Dergoz.

They haven't even noticed the strange lumps in my bra, which I'm pretty grateful for, considering my escape plan hinges on me getting my newly enlarged chest into their bunker.

"Why, exactly, do you need me?" I doubt they'll tell me, but it's worth a —

"To control the Brute, and for our breeding program, obviously," the first Roth answers blithely.

"Oh good," I wheeze, "that's great."

"The other human females have not been nearly so compliant."

"I can imagine," I muster, and the Roth flank me, nudging me forward and into the blazing sun. "How exactly did you find ah, all these human females?" If they're going to talk, I'm going to ask them. Michelle would be proud!

That's a lie. Michelle would shit her pants if she knew I was willingly being taken by these assholes. For their breeding program. I swallow against the nauseated, dizzy feeling that grips me.

"There was a Federation crew that attempted to attack a Roth warship outside Earth space."

"And the crew was all female?"

"No, there were males too, but our people killed them."

"Of course," I say, tamping down my anger. This is the Roth I expected. The murderous ones.

"You are quite sensible for a human female."

"Oh, I'm full of surprises," I say easily, walking with them towards the hatch. Horatio pads along beside me, earning several consternated glances from my Roth honor guard. Dishonor guard. Whichever.

"So you are not opposed to being bred by the Roth? Tested for breeding compatibility?"

The second Roth's face is full of hope, and I tamp down my disgust.

"Ehhhh," I manage.

"That is not a no," the first Roth says happily. "Perhaps you can persuade the other human females to be more compliant."

"That's certainly an idea," I agree. "A real idea. Just out there, in the open."

"I am so pleased we have found you." He throws the latch on the hatch, and I ignore the intelligent part of my brain screaming to shove him down the hole. Horatio mewls, and I bend, picking him up with a grunt.

"Did you gain weight?" I ask him. "Sheesh."

"Will you be able to climb down and hold that creature at the same time?"

"Oh yeah, sure," I say easily. "Piece of cake. Humans are great with their hands."

The Roth's eyes widen in surprise, a slow smile growing across his face. Maybe that wasn't the right thing to say. Too late now!

"To the Brute!" I say, wrapping one arm around Horatio's thick, furry body, and following the first Roth down the ladder. "That guy just loves making people eat their own guts, huh?"

Sure, they want me for baby-making purposes, which, honestly, it seems half the galaxy does, but they haven't been horrible. I was expecting pure horror. Maybe some light torture.

Instead, what I found is two grey aliens who act like total himbos and seem to want a family as bad as any hard-up Suevan Warlord.

My mind rationally knows they're the enemy... but are they really that different from the Suevans? Or even Reif, the Arco?

If it weren't for what they did to Earth, I might believe that.

Instead, I hold the cat close and my fear closer, climbing down the ladder one handed and praying Mr. Acid-Spit Horatio doesn't decide to bite me.

But he doesn't, settling into me and purring with delight at our newest adventure.

Glad one of us is happy about it, at least.

DERGOZ

I LAY on the cell floor, soaking in the heat, drifting off and trying to let my shoulder wound heal. It appears the pulse tore right through the muscle, and while it's tender, it seems to be healing nicely.

All in all, it could be much worse.

Like if Bex were to have been captured with us. That would be much, much worse.

No sooner has the thought flitted through my thick skull than I scent her.

I open my eyes, studying the ambient light source overhead. It must be a memory, the indelible fragrance of my mate imprinted on my brain, triggered by the merest thought of her.

The plastitech door blocks most of the sound, but it allows me to see out, and frosts for privacy when the occupants are asleep. It is a very thoughtful prison design, and I can't help but wonder at why the Roth have bothered with it at all.

The sweet scent grows stronger, and fear strikes through me.

I sit up, wincing as the movement tugs at my wound, and stand as soon as she comes into view.

Ree-becca.

My wife, my mate, her hideous alien pet at her heels, being escorted into the prison hallway by two Roth, who seem to be… smiling at her?

She chatters away, her clever gaze taking everything in, missing nothing as she scans the space.

I may not know this female as well as I would like, but even I, who has misjudged her again and again, can tell she is up to something. It is in the calculating way she soaks in her surroundings, in the too-confident strut of her walk. I only hope it will be enough to keep her safe, where I have so clearly failed.

She stops in front of my cell, her mouth moving as she says something I can't understand to the Roth guards.

The cell behind her lights up as one of the human females moves forward, toward the plastitech door, watching the newest arrival.

Bex turns as the light falls across the hallway, and her body goes tense, then softens as the guards note the shift in her.

My heart hammers against my chest with worry for her.

When she turns back to me, her eyes are lit with a manic rage. Beside her, Horatio puffs up to twice his size.

The door hisses open, and the guards aim their pistols at me. I raise my manacled hands in the air, trying to show I pose no threat. The guard's faces are full of fear, the acrid scent of it filling the small cell, only to be quickly filtered away.

I want to rip their arms off and shove them up their—

"Are you certain you feel safe with this monster?"

I snarl in response, every inch the very monster they fear me to be. Bex narrows her eyes, clearly furious with me.

Not as furious as I am with myself.

My eyes skate over her, looking for evidence of any injury. Her breasts look… strange, and when I see the angry red marks on her still-bound wrists, my throat closes up in worry.

I did that to her.

I *am* a monster.

"He's no more monstrous than any one of us," Bex says evenly, though her expression promises murder. Maybe my murder.

I'm so ridden with guilt that it takes me a moment to mark her words.

"You would think I am monstrous if you knew what I planned to do with the Roth behind you," I growl, my voice guttural and low.

"Nah, these two? They're sweethearts. Aren't you, boys? Thanks for bringing me to my husband." Her grin turns from kind to evil as she glances back at me. "We have a lot to discuss."

"Yeaaaaaaaah," Horatio screams. I wince at the sound, then do a double take. Why hasn't she killed the guards with her horrible animal? That thing could easily take them down, and then… and then every Roth in this base would be aware of the problem.

She glides into the cell, poised and beautiful and very clearly incandescent with anger.

Every step she takes towards me sets me on fire, something rising in me, wanting to meet her head on, wanting to watch her explode as I trail kisses down her pretty neck.

The door slides shut behind her, locking us in together.

"What have you done?" I ask softly, nearly choking on the words. "Why are you friendly with them?"

She takes another step closer, closing the distance between us.

Her delicate hands slide up my bare torso.

"They're watching, so we're going to give them a little show. For the record, I am furious with you. Livid. Beyond mad. But I'm not going to just abandon you." She molds herself against me, her soft stomach pressing against the hard bulge in my pants. I bite back a groan. "Unlike you did to me." She flutters her eyelashes at me, but her mouth is a grim line.

"Your wrists are hurt."

Her expression softens slightly. "They are."

"I did that to you." Fury races through me, an impotent rage I have only myself to blame for.

"Not exactly." Her adorable nose scrunches, and I cannot fight my delight at having her in my arms, even though our situation is dire. Even though she must hate me now.

"Then how? Was it the Roth? I will rip their limbs from their bodies and beat them bloody with them—"

"You know, maybe it's better if I don't tell you what happened." Her hands slide across my neck, her breasts rubbing along my chest. I groan, unable to stop the sound from coming out. Something hard scrapes across my scales, and I blink, my tail slapping against the back wall of the cell.

"What is this? What is wrong with your—"

"Shut up and kiss me," Bex snarls, her hands tugging my face down.

As soon as her mouth meets mine, all thought flees my mind. The world stops turning, the very stars themselves shine brighter, spangling the endless tapestry of space as they smile upon her.

I have done my best to ruin the thin thread between us, to unravel what could have been magic. I have acted like a fool, over and over again, and yet here this small female stands, her soft lips against mine, her tiny hands tugging my face to hers, her breasts hard against my chest—

Wait.

I pull back, dizzy with need and trying to sort my thoughts out.

"Are they gone?" she asks in a low voice.

"Who? What?"

"The Roth. Are they still watching?"

"No—"

"Good. We need to be ready when our evac gets here. Though we weren't counting on additional bodies to rescue… Where's Reif?"

"What do you mean, an evac? You called for backup?"

"Listen," she scowls, irritation crawling across her face as she wiggles past me, putting her hands on the wall and thrusting her ass out as she places her ear on it.

I lean close to the wall, trying to figure out what it is she wants me to listen to.

"Closer," she says, beckoning me with one finger.

Anticipation grips me. Perhaps she will kiss me again. Perhaps she will do more than kiss me… I lean even closer to her, putting my ear near her lips.

"YOU DON'T GET TO JUDGE THE CALL I MADE AFTER YOU FUCKED ME OVER AND LEFT ME FOR DEAD!"

I wince, clapping my hand over my ear as it rings from the force of her voice.

"Yeaaaaaaaah!" Horatio agrees loudly.

"Thanks, Horatio, I knew I could count on you to have my back."

"So you *are* mad," I say slowly, scratching my chin. This female is the most confusing, confounding, bewitching creature I have ever met. I have gone from nearly despising her to being utterly obsessed with her in a matter of days.

"Mad? Mad?! I am fucking furious. Livid. Beyond angry. Nuclear. Apocalyptic. You name it, I'm there."

"Why did you kiss me, then?"

"For one, to sell the story I told those dumbass Roth. Which, by the way, is true, considering I am married to you! And two, because even though I'm super fucking pissed off at you, I still like you, you big scaly himbo lizardman."

"I am not a lizard."

"Of course, *that's* the part you get stuck on." She throws her hands in the air and makes a sound of disgust.

I catch her forearms in my hands, careful not to touch the tender red sores on her wrists. "It pains me to see your skin marred. It hurts me to know I have hurt you. I am sorry that I betrayed you, and I am sorry that you are caught here with me now… And I am awed that you still carry affection for me."

"Well, I don't want you to die." Her lips twitch slightly, then curve down into a frown.

"That is a start." Not a great one, but a start.

"And I hate that I had to listen to you get shot after you left me helpless with nothing but a kitty to defend myself with."

"That creature is hardly defenseless." I cast a glance back at Horatio.

"Yeaaaaaaaah!" he screams at me. I shake my head, cringing at the sheer amount of teeth in the thing's mouth. It should be physically impossible for anything to have that many teeth.

"It doesn't matter, Dergoz, that's not the point. You can't just tie me up because you're worried about me getting hurt. You can't wrap me in bubble wrap or put me on a pedestal or any of that nonsense. I am who I am, and that person is a damn good tech. I am useful, you fucker, and you left me tied up."

"I would very much like to be a fucker right now." My words come out on a growl, surprising us both.

"Argh!" she says, turning from me and rubbing her hands on the smooth cell wall.

I squint at her. "It's unlike you to turn down sex."

"For one, it would be very public sex," she says, waving at the clear plastitech door. "Oh, there's Reif." She pauses long enough to give him a little wave and a thumbs-up. "Why is he staring at me like that?"

"Probably because you just told him you want to put your hand in his asshole."

"Oh." She stares at her thumb. "That would do it. What was I saying, again?"

"You were telling me why we cannot have sex, even though I scent your need. Even though everything in me is screaming at me to take you right here, right now, and rut you like the Brute I am."

Her breath catches slightly, but she shakes her head. "No. I'm angry with you and I don't want to have sex right now."

"Your body tells a different story."

"Oh really? Where was this great body language translator when you were tying me up, huh?!" Her hands lift the hem of her shirt, exposing her soft belly.

My cock jerks at the sight.

"What are you doing?" I ask. "If you do not want me to plunge my cock into your velvet depths, why are you teasing me?"

"It's not about you, you big green hunk." She huffs in distress, tugging the tank over her shoulders. "Block me from view. Act like you're doing me from behind or something."

I stare at her for a long moment, and she sighs, pulling me behind her, where my cock presses against the firm round of her ass.

"Fuck, Ree-becca, I could spill right now."

"Do what you need to, but you should know I'm doing this to get us all out of here alive."

When she pulls at the band of the undergarment binding her breasts, I snarl in anticipation, bracing myself against the wall of the cell. But instead of pulling out her heavy breasts, she produces…

Equipment parts?

"That explains what I felt when you wantonly rubbed against me."

"Oh, is that right? I'm wanton now? Who's doing the rubbing now?"

"If you are wanton, then I am a slave to my lust," I whisper in her ear, noting with satisfaction as a small tremor rocks her body. "I am out of my mind with desire for you, and I care nothing about those who watch. All I know is my need. All I want to know is your body around mine, your mouth saying my name as you come around my cock."

"Oh," she says softly, then clears her throat. "That's nice."

"There is nothing nice about it, Ree-becca. For you I *would* be monstrous. For you I would burn the world and everything in it, just for you to forgive me. Just for one look. One kiss."

"That's, ah, that's hot. But unnecessary." Her hands are sliding over the walls, and I realize she's searching for something. She's not just teasing me with her tight, thick ass against my cock and her breasts nearly spilling from her undergarments.

The little zoleh is setting something up to allow us to escape.

"You are full of surprises." The words are soft against her ear, and she quivers slightly, her fingers still probing at the wall.

"Well," her voice is breathless, and it sends a fresh surge of lust through me. "Any minute now—"

The lights shut off.

"There it is," she finishes. "I told them to give us some privacy, fluttered my lashes and told them human females are shy."

"You do not want them to watch me fuck you? Because I am losing control, sweet Ree-becca. I am close to showing you exactly how careless I can be." It's odd that the Roth are willing to follow her directions at all, but my brain can only focus on so many things, and right now, all my brain power solely revolves around the need to make her mine. To mate her.

To show her exactly how sorry I am.

"Ah," her voice comes out a squeak. "I… You're forgetting I'm still mad at you."

"Your lips say one thing, but the delicious aroma of your cunt tells me another." I slide my hand lower, until my talons are just under the waistband of her pants.

"You are making this much harder than it has to be," she says.

"Oh, it is very hard for you already," I purr, pressing more firmly into her heat.

"There," she gasps, and for a moment, I smile in satisfaction, until I realize she's managed to pop open a slick compartment in the wall.

"What are you doing?" I say, my cock bobbing as I try to rein myself in. My fangs brush against the tender skin under her ear, and she arches against me as she pulls several components from her undergarments.

"I figured these cells were a lot like ones they use on the Roth ships. We dismantled a few, reverse engineered them, after the invasion. They have a flaw, and that is their power source can be hacked remotely, from a panel almost exactly like this one."

"That is a rather large flaw," I manage, awed by her skill. A fresh wave of guilt pushes through me. I should have brought her with me.

"Well," she says darkly, all heat leaving her voice. "Most people who spend time in their cells don't live to tell tales of what it's like."

"You will be safe with me."

"Yeaaaaaaaah!!!" Horatio screams.

Bex chuckles into the dark. "I can't see as well without light as you. Tell me what you see."

"Light blue squares, orange rectangles," I tell her.

"Show me," she commands.

I take her hands in mine, moving them carefully over the hidden panel in the wall. Quickly, her delicate fingers work over the sophisticated Roth tech as she pries several pieces apart, reconnecting others quickly. "You're too quiet," she admonishes me.

"What do you mean?"

"You're supposed to be fucking me like a monster, remember?"

I growl loudly into her ear. "Is that what you want, sweet human," I say loudly. "You want to be fucked by a monster? I will slam this cock into your wet cunt, over and over again, until you come all over me."

Her body shakes, and for a moment I think I've aroused her as she concentrates, until I realize she's stifling a giggle.

"Why do you laugh?" Hurt and bad memories swell in me.

"I'm sorry," she whispers. "That was really good. It's just… It's funny. We're stuck in a prison cell and I'm trying to hack our way out of it and we have an alien cat who keeps screaming and you're doing a really good job dirty talking and—" Her fingers fly over the panel, and it glows light green for a half second.

"There," she sighs. "That's as good as I can get it." She strokes the wall, and the slick covering slides back into place, hiding it from view.

"Oh," I say, emboldened by her praise, "I will give it to you good. I will give it to you so good and you will ask for more."

"I am still mad at you," she manages, though her ass rubs against my cock beguilingly.

"Then tell me to stop," I snarl. My hands slide from hers, up her muscled forearms, the soft curves of her biceps.

I pause, waiting for her to say no. Waiting for her to say yes.

"Dergoz," she says, need coloring her voice.

"If you are too angry with me, I will stop."

"Don't—" She tilts her head back, relaxing into my chest. "But this doesn't mean I forgive you."

"Of course, it doesn't," I tell her, but now? Now I am determined to win her forgiveness. To earn it. To learn her body until she responds exactly the way I want her to. "I will have to prove to you that I am worth forgiving."

My hands reach the round tops of her breasts, and her breath comes quicker, her arousal scent deepening. I dip them inside the soft fabric that binds them, rolling her nipples between my thumb and forefingers as she gasps at the contact.

Snarling, I half-bite, half-kiss her neck, utterly undone by the ample heaviness in my hands, by her sweet scent and even sweeter submission.

I keep one hand on her breast, where the beat of her heart is, luxuriating in the feel of her, and slide the other one down her stomach.

Her breath catches as I stroke the small thatch of coarse hair between her legs. When she lets out a small moan as my fingertips glide effortlessly through her wet heat, I snarl in appreciation.

"So fucking wet already. You say you're mad, but you want this, do you not? You want my big cock inside you."

"Yes," she groans. "I'm so fucking mad. I want you."

I stop leashing myself. Extracting my hands from her, I rip her pants and undergarment to her ankles in one swift movement, mine following in the next second.

She shivers against my body, and I lick the side of her neck, eliciting a moan that makes me impossibly hard.

"I am going to take you now," I tell her, and it's all the warning I give before I plunge deep inside her.

By the goddess, she feels… incredible. Wet and hot and so fucking tight. I pause, trying to wrestle some semblance of control over myself.

She bucks against me, her ass flush with my hips.

"Bex, my Ree-becca," I say softly, affection coursing through me. The sight of her ample ass is fucking everything, and I squeeze it as my cock throbs inside her.

"Dergoz," she says, bouncing slightly on her toes. I'm having to crouch to take her like this, and she's balancing on the tips of her toes, sopping wet and delicious. My xof vibrates, making her round cheeks quiver with it.

"Let me help you, my sweet," I grit out, and then use all of my willpower to pull out of her perfect cunt. She moans at the loss of it, and I nearly spill a rope of cum across her ass in that very instant. I flip her around so that I can see her sweet face, and then lift her.

"I would make this good for you," I tell her, and she writhes as I kneel, putting her legs across my shoulders. "I am going to make you come now, do you understand?"

"I don't forgive you," she pants.

"Not yet," I say, and with a wicked grin, delighting in each small bead of sweat that shines atop her brow, I bury my face in her delectable cunt. One long lick draws a breathy moan out of her.

I am a cruel male, though. I know exactly where she wants me, know exactly how to make her scream my name, to prove to any Roth who listens that I am bringing my mate the greatest pleasure she's ever known… but I don't. Instead, I tease her, flicking my rough tongue around the bud of her pleasure, letting her writhe against my mouth, coating me in her juices.

"Please, Dergoz," she says, her voice faint and reedy.

"If I do not have your forgiveness, then how can I make you come?" I growl, pinning her more surely against the wall and my body.

"Please, let me come," she says, tugging at my hair, trying anything she can to get me to lavish affection on the small bud of her pleasure. "I'm so close."

"Are you still angry?" I ask, then shove my tongue roughly into her opening, tasting my precum and her desire all at once. It makes me fucking vicious. It makes me want her more. It makes me want to fill her up and make her scream my name until she all but blacks out from the pleasure of it.

"I'm so fucking angry," she says, trying to increase the pressure, trying to rub against me.

"You won't relent, will you?"

"Not when you're being an asshole," she says.

And just like that, an idea comes to me, and I smile wickedly between tantalizingly slow licks. I want to fill her completely. I want to leave no room for her anger. I want there to be nothing but me.

There's a reason they call me the Brute, and she does't know the half of it.

Slowly, I run my talon-less fingertip around her wetness, lubricating it. She moans, and my desire heightens, everything pulling tighter.

"You're mine," I growl savagely, tracing my finger delicately along the skin between her vagina and her ass. She clenches, moaning, as I carefully penetrate her back opening, using my tongue to fuck her cunt at the same time.

"Say you're mine," I grit out between thrusts.

"Yours, yours," she chants. "Oh God, Dergoz, I'm so fucking close."

"Say it again," I say, licking my way back to her clit, feeling her lose control, dangerously close to losing it myself.

"I'm yours, I'm yours, Dergoz, all yours. Please, please, please—"

I suck hard at her clit, and she screams—*screams*—my name, the sound echoing off the walls of the cell.

I can't wait anymore.

I want to be back inside her. I want to cum hard inside her.

So I lay her on her back as the climax continues to roll through her, and I slam into her cunt with the fevered intent of a male possessed.

TWENTY-FIVE

BEX

I CAN HARDLY BREATHE. I am done thinking, evidently. All that matters is the green sex god ramming into me, his huge, thick cock so deep that I can't catch my breath.

And the thing on top, his xof, vibrating, hit my clit *just* right.

I come again as it makes contact, and Dergoz slows down, his tail rubbing against my ankle possessively as he grinds against me, using his vibrating equipment to its absolute full potential.

"Are you still mad at me?" he snaps out, his voice a gravelly rasp. "Tell me you're still mad now," he commands.

"Unnhhh-huh," I moan, arching up into him, chasing another fucking orgasm as his body works into me, deeper, fuller, faster.

His mouth catches the tip of my breast, one arm hooking around my back as he sucks on it through the fabric of my bra.

"Fuck," I moan, my entire body clenching as another orgasm starts to tear through me. I don't even care who can hear me. I don't even care if someone is watching us.

I might even like that idea a little bit.

"I can feel you coming around me, my sweet Ree-becca," he says, picking up the pace again. "Your wet honey coats my legs. I will be sticky with your release, and I will fill you up with mine. I think you like this, yes? I think you like that we might be found out. I'll have to remember this."

In the next instant, his body jerks, as though the thought of his cum inside me with someone watching sent him over the edge. His fun little sex toy vibrates even harder, and I scream again, another orgasm cresting right on the heels of the last.

When we're both finally still, his weight heavy on me, his mouth buried in my hair, I'm shaking like a leaf.

"Yeaaaaaah!!" yells Horatio from somewhere in the cell.

"Not now," I say groggily, completely spent. Utterly relaxed. Utterly unconcerned that we're in a sweaty heap on the floor of a Roth prison, thanks to the multiple, super strong orgasms this male dragged from my body.

Tenderly, Dergoz pushes a strand of my sweaty hair from my forehead, then kisses along my brow.

I can't help the tiny smile that forms on my lips.

"You are not laughing," he says. I can't make out his face in the dark, but there's a sense of wonder to his words that makes my heart squeeze, just a little.

"That was the best sex of my life," I tell him honestly.

"So you are no longer mad," he says agreeably.

"No, I'm still furious with you. But I can say with utmost certainty that if you keep that up, I will have a hard time staying mad."

"Good," he says, and to my shock, his cock begins to harden inside me again, the vibrating starting up all over.

"I can—" What I can't do is get the words out, because no sooner does he start moving again then another wave of pleasure builds inside of me. "Oh, Dergoz, oh my God, oh, oh…"

I hold tight to his back, matching his speed with my own, and this time, we both come quickly, within a matter of minutes, the time blurring by like stars in warp.

"I should clean you up," he says.

"Okay," I agree, waiting for the feel of cloth against my too-sensitive pussy.

Instead, his hot tongue lashes against me, and I gasp as he laps up the liquid between my legs.

"Oh, shit," I moan, my hands finding his hair. "I don't think I can take much more of this."

"You can take it, and you will take it, and you will forgive me," he grates out, working me so hard with his tongue and his fingers that it's all I can do to hold on for dear life as he feasts on me.

"I can't, I can't, I can't," I pant, and he redoubles his efforts, his fingers making slick sounds as he fucks me with them hard, his mouth working my clit like an expert.

It's literally everything I've ever wanted, this huge hunk of muscled male licking me within an inch of my life, pinning my hips with one hand and holding my ankle with his heavy tail.

"Fuck," I moan, completely unable to resist the pleasure ratcheting inside me.

"There it is," he says in appreciation. "That's a good mate, letting me drink your arousal as you gush around my tongue."

"Uh-huh," I manage, pulling my legs up and then falling limp onto my side.

He curls next to me, licking his fingers. I can't see him, but self-satisfaction and male pride practically rolls off him.

"You look well-sated, mate," he says approvingly, gently brushing hair from my face, then tugging me into his body. Carefully, he pulls my pants back up. "Are you very tired?"

"Unghuhh," I manage, unable to form words.

"Can you tell me your plan?"

"Surprise," I say.

"You want it to be a surprise?"

"Eh," I say, then a yawn cracks my jaw before I can say anything else. I don't really want it to be a surprise, in fact, it makes a hell of a lot more sense to tell him than to keep it a secret.

"I don't want secrets between us," I say instead, and that admission, more than anything, shocks me.

He stills, then his hand resumes stroking my bare arm, lulling me into extreme relaxation. Melting me. As though I could be any more relaxed after what we just did.

Whew! I was totally correct to lust after him, good job me.

"You are still upset that I left you tied up," he says quietly.

"Yes. Though, if you tied me up later, for fun, I would be totally into that." Great, all my inhibitions have been completely fucked out of me. I clear my throat. "But, I mean, yes. Yes, that was horrible. Awful."

"And yet you seek me for comfort now. You are a puzzling creature."

"Eh. I contain multitudes." Of cum. I swallow the thought, then a laugh spills out of me.

"I will make it up to you," he promises, bowing his head to kiss my shoulder. "I do not want there to be secrets between us either. I do not want to be the reason you are hurt, or angry, or..." His body goes tense.

"Or?" I prompt.

"Or trapped in a Roth prison."

"Well, it's a good thing I have a rescue planned, then."

"And how do you plan to do that, when you are trapped in here? Your system hack may open the cell doors," he says quietly, "but it will not disable the Roth guards."

"No, but that's why I'm counting on Nydo and the Gladiator and Michelle and whoever else they send to bust us out of this bitch."

"Why is it a bitch?" The confusion is clear in his voice. "It is genderless. It is a prison."

"You know, that's a good question. Maybe when I have a functioning brain cell we can deconstruct the usage of that language when applied to inanimate objects." I'm rambling, and I can't quite stop myself.

"Why Nydo?" he asks cautiously.

"Because subterfuge, obviously."

"I think I see," he says.

"All I see are the back of my eyelids," I tell him, and before I can finish that thought, I'm drifting off to his heat around me. Horatio curls up at my feet, purring and furry and warm, and it's all I need to pass out completely.

———

Too bright. The hum of the overhead lights is too much, too artificial for my myza room, and for a moment, I'm completely thrown.

Dergoz pulls me tighter against him, shushing me quietly and jerking his head toward the clear cell partition.

Across the prison hall, the human females beat their fists against their cell door. A cloud disperses from the ceiling, and I watch in abject horror as they begin to cough, then slump against the plastitech barrier. It isn't until I see their chests rising and falling evenly that I realize they're just asleep.

The knowledge doesn't do much to quell the revulsion turning my stomach.

"They are asleep," Dergoz confirms, his tone quiet and shocked, too. "Do not say anything."

"Did you know they could do that?" I hiss. "I didn't plan for that. The cells on their warships don't have any kind of aerosol configuration."

Roth guards stream into the cell, followed by what appear to be medical personnel, Roth males, like everyone else, who carefully prod and poke the women with devices.

"They're conducting tests. Should be painless, mostly." Dergoz runs his hands down my arms, and I shake against him. "Do not be afraid, my sweet. I will protect you."

"I'm not afraid," I say, and maybe that's stupid, but I'm not. "I'm fucking furious. Those are people. Federation officers... and they're just... they're just—"

"Treating them like broodmares," he finishes for me, his voice troubled.

"What time is it?" I ask, my toes twitching. Horatio stirs at my feet, then clambers on top of my chest, purring like a motor.

"It is hard to say. You slept a long while though. It could be night. I have lost my sense of time, as deep underground as we appear to be."

"How is your shoulder?" If we have to run, I want him to be as fast as he can be.

"Fine. Healing. How are your wrists?"

"Fine." They are too, mostly. Sore, for sure, but fine. In fact, a quick look tells me they're already healing very well, much faster than I would have anticipated.

"I cannot apologize enough."

"We don't have time for any more apologizing," I say, watching the Roth flit around from woman to woman, taking measurements and tests and recording them on their tablets. They appear buoyed by the responses, one even grinning and clapping another on the shoulder.

That makes me even more sick.

I don't think I want to know what they're celebrating.

"We need to up our timeline," I say thickly. I can barely make out Reif, pacing in front of his cell door, one of his fins bedraggled where it hangs off his shoulder. "I don't want to be on the receiving end of that spray."

"I will kill them," Dergoz says succinctly. "I will rip their arms off and feed them to them, joint by joint."

"As romantic as that is, hubby, I'm not sure we're going to have time for any appendage force-feeding."

"What is a hubby?"

"Husband? It's short for it. It's kind of a gross nickname though, just thought I'd try to lighten the mood—"

Shouting sounds from above, and we both tip our heads to the ceiling, listening. Horatio stands up, his fur puffing out, and hisses, showing off his poisonous teeth. Too many teeth, honestly.

"You were right," I tell Dergoz. "About Horatio."

"I am not sure I want to hear this," he grumbles.

"He is poisonous," I tell him cheerily. "But look at it this way, he's going to fight on our side, and the Roth don't have a clue, the big grey losers." I frown as the noise grows closer, louder. "Surely they aren't here yet? It's only been one night…" Unless.

"Dergoz… you don't think they…"

"They must have drugged us too," Dergoz hisses, his tail slapping the floor behind him. "Get dressed, it's time to move."

"We're going to have to take a bunch of unconscious Federation women with us, too," I moan, scrubbing a hand over my face. "This is not how I envisioned this going when I called in the cavalry."

"They are going to be mounted?" Dergoz says, the words laced with confusion.

"No… though maybe that's not a terrible idea. Element of surprise and all that."

"I do not think mounts would do well underground."

"Okay, this conversational derailment is over. I need you to block me from view while I trigger the doors to unlock."

"And then I will pull them limb from limb—"

I hold up a hand, silencing what I'm sure is going to become a stream of even gorier threats. "Honestly, Dergoz, these fuckers aren't my favorites. But unless we have time for you to beat them senseless with their own fists, let's just concentrate on escaping."

"As you wish." He pauses, his fang pressing down on his lower lip as he studies me. "Does my violence disturb you? It is why they call me monstrous. A brute."

I grin at him, then press a long kiss to his mouth. "I fucking love it. I just need you to focus."

"So you aren't mad at me anymore?" He asks, his brows lifting, diamond-pupil eyes expanding slightly.

I nearly laugh at his boyish tone, but instead, I kiss him again.

"That's a no?"

"Oh, I'm still mad, but I'm sure you can persuade me to forgive you as soon as we are safe."

"Then we must act doubly quickly, because I am ready to persuade you immediately."

Something vibrates against my hip, and I roll my eyes, my lips quirking into a smile. "Escape first, fuck later."

"Deal," Dergoz says quickly. "Should we pretend to fuck while you hack their system?"

"Er," I say, "maybe—"

But it's too late, he's shoved me against the back wall, grinding up against me, wrapping my ponytail around his fist as I gasp in surprise. My cheeks heat, and I struggle to remember what the hell I'm even doing.

"Your vibrating is distracting me."

"No, it is arousing you."

"Same difference." I run my hands down the wall again, finding the seam more quickly this time.

"Your words make no sense, but I find them titillating all the same," his breath fans across my ear, and I twitch my head away from him.

"I'm trying to save our asses here," I mutter, accessing the panel and fiddling with the controls.

The sound of plas pulses rockets through even the thick plas-titech cell door, and I nearly fall as the ground rumbles. Dergoz's hands keep me upright, my heart thudding double time against my chest.

Sweat slicks the back of my neck as I fumble with the components. I have to do this. I have to be able to activate the emergency shut off that will allow all the cells to open. I have to get out of here, I have to get the rest of the humans out of here, and the Arco males, too.

And Dergoz.

My throat constricts, my clammy hands slipping over the alien tech as I try to input the correct sequence. If done correctly, it will overload the mechanism and trigger the emergency release without locking the whole facility down. Luckily, there's no life support system to worry about here like there is on a ship in space, but I'd rather not be plunged into darkness around hostiles all the same.

"What I wouldn't give for a fookie right now," I say. I must've picked up Niki's bad sugar habits on the long trip to Sueva, because suddenly, all I can think about is a warm chocolate chip cookie.

"Then slide your pants down and let me thrust inside your sweet cunt."

I pause, incredulous, and look over my shoulder at the big Suevan whose cock is already hard against my ass. "The treat. The cookie. The faux-cookie. That is not what…"

"Are you sure?" he purrs, rubbing my ass with his thick-fingered hand.

"Later," I whisper-shout at him, annoyed and turned-on all at once and somehow also trying not to laugh, despite the seriousness of our predicament.

Finally, the panel sparks slightly, the metal pieces I planted last night to make the brute force electric overload easier melting as I jab the energy reactor in just the right place.

Sweat drips down my nose, sizzling on the now hot panel, which I immediately drop.

Noise explodes through the cell, and Dergoz swings around, pressing me up against the wall and his back.

Protecting me.

Awww. It's so sweet.

Oh. The reason I'm crammed into the wall and Dergoz's huge tail is because, thankfully, my little trick with the panel worked. Our plastitech cell door is gone, disappeared into the floor, along with all the other cell doors.

Reif surges from his cell, the Roth who were still working on the unconscious human women are caught unawares as he bears down on them.

I blink, utterly in awe and slightly scared of his prowess. He doesn't just beat the Roth, he demolishes them. Well, figuratively, that is. He knocks them unconscious, and they slump to the floor next to the female captives.

No sooner have I adjusted to our new reality of almost-freedom than all hell breaks loose.

Plasma fire ricochets off the ceiling, knocking one of the ambient lights out.

I throw my hands in the air, completely frustrated. "Oh, great, so I went to all that trouble just so some asshole with a gun could take out the lights? Fucking perfect."

"You were incredible," Dergoz says.

I squeak as he grabs me, carrying me bridal style out of our prison cell. Blue and pink plasma pulses light up the now-dim corridor. Grey-skinned and uniformed Roth block the only exit, shouting commands and clearly fraying at the onslaught.

And then something red and orange flares, and the Roth that are guarding the entryway to the prison cells gasp in one voice. Heat bursts from the entrance, a warm glow that crackles licking past us, lighting up the entire cell block.

I strain, trying to catch sight of whatever this weapon is the Suevans have brought.

I've never seen anything like it.

When Nydo rounds the corner, I choke.

It's not a weapon.

It's *him*. He is on fire. Literally on fire. His dark hair burns blue and orange, flames caressing his gray skin and strange symbols. Orange eyes glow, two embers in a face that I will never forget.

And it doesn't seem to bother him, not one bit.

The Roth guards, on the other hand, fall to their knees, their weapons forgotten, prostrate before him.

"What the fuck?" Dergoz mutters, his arms tight around me.

"My sentiments exactly, ya big green beefcake," I agree.

"Bow before the rightful king! Bow before the heir to the throne!" One of the Roth yells, and the plasma pulses stop entirely as Nydo strides down the corridor to us.

"Do you require assistance?" he asks, looking downright irritated at all the fuss he's caused.

"Rightful king?" I manage. The bitchy effect is somewhat lost, considering I'm being held like a baby by my thick AF husband.

"We all have our secrets. Mine was too dangerous to even think of." His gaze swings to the cell full of unconscious women, and his lip curls. "They would slaughter my whole family if the Overlord knew my bloodline still existed."

"What's with the fire?"

"It is one of the great mysteries of our kind," he intones solemnly.

"He's an energy manipulator," Dergoz explains. "It's very rare."

Nydo scowls at him.

"I did not know of this," he finally says, gesturing to the sleeping women.

"Yeah, well, this place is just full of surprises," I say.

Horatio screams, and guilt winds through me. Did I really forget about my adorable little monster cat in all the hubbub?

Yes. I sure did.

"Horatio, you cutie little sweet pea pumpkin head, don't yell at Mama. You're coming with us."

Dergoz gives a long-suffering sigh as the cat-alien winds between his legs.

"We cannot leave the human females here," Nydo says. He sucks in a huge breath, the flames around him burning brighter and hotter, the dark swirls on his skin appearing to flicker.

"No shit, Sherlock," I snap.

"Don't be rude to him," a female voice says softly. "He's helped. As soon as he turned on his, er, energy manipulation, the rest of the Roth went peacefully."

"Most of them," another Suevan says.

My eyes go wide as I take Michelle and Alvez, who walk towards us through the still kneeling Roth. They aren't quite touching, not exactly, but there's a tension between them that's thick enough it would take a hot knife to cut through.

Or maybe just a healthy dose of Nydo's firepower.

"You came with him," I say stupidly.

Michelle arches an eyebrow at me. "I wasn't just going to leave you here. Someone with half a brain needed to show up to help."

"You have much more than half a brain," Alvez says, his gaze raking over her.

Dergoz sets me down on my feet, and Horatio immediately puts his front paws on my hips, and I pick him up. The alien cat drapes himself over my shoulders, purring away like a little vibrating fur cape.

Michelle's nose wrinkles. "What is that thing?"

"It's a cat."

"No, it's not."

"It is."

"Is not."

"It's a poisonous divimenton. An alien youngling," Nydo answers.

"Well, that sounds perfectly safe, since it's a baby and all," Michelle sighs.

"He's my baby now, aren't you, Horatio?" I ask him, scratching him under his chin.

"Yeaaaaaaaaah!" Horatio yowls.

Alvez shudders.

"Why does that thing sound like it's saying yeaaaaaaaaah?"

"That's just what he sounds like. And his *name* is Horatio."

"Like that old show set in Miami? That guy with the glasses and the horrible puns?"

"I don't know what you're talking about," I lie.

"Mmhmm," Michelle says skeptically. She glances over at the women passed out in the cell, her expression darkening. "We might not have room for all of these women on our ship."

Reif steps out from the cell, and Alvez pushes Michelle behind him, snarling threateningly.

Uh-huh. Looks like there's a little bit to unpack there, all right.

"I have room on my ship," Reif says. "I can take them to my planet. Arco."

"Who the heck is this guy?" Michelle asks, scrunching her nose.

"An Arco," Nydo says darkly, his flames burning brighter.

I sigh. If these idiots continue bowing up to each other, I'm going to need an overhead sprinkler system to bring them back to their senses.

"If everyone doesn't calm down, I'm going to sic Horatio on you."

"Yeeaaaaaaaah!" Horatio agrees. One of his tails slaps against my mouth, and I cough against the sudden hair assault on my nostrils.

Michelle starts to laugh, but it quickly turns into a cough as Alvez shoots her a pained expression.

Reif glances between us all, taking our measure. "I can help escort the human females to Sueva, too. There, perhaps, they can choose if they would like to stay on your planet, or go to Arco."

"Or with the Roth," Nydo says darkly, a fresh font of flame sizzling down his shoulders and arms.

"Yeah, I don't think they're going to want to go with the Roth after what your boys did to them."

Nydo stiffens, his lip curling in disgust. "What did they do to them?"

"Oh, you know, a little scientific breeding testing against their will after they were drugged." I flutter my eyelashes.

Nydo snarls, and Dergoz takes a menacing step toward him.

"This is the work of the Roth Overlord," he growls, his eyes glowing even brighter.

Shit, he's scary like this. My throat gets tight, my mind telling me to run.

Thank fuck none of the other Roth can do that energy manipulation shit. Earth would have been smoking ruins.

Michelle glances between us, her intelligent eyes calculating, and I just know she's working out exactly how to manipulate everyone, just like the Federation trained their best intel analysts to do. Look for weaknesses. Look for levers.

Use them.

"Holy shitballs," I exclaim excitedly as it hits me. "You can understand them? Your translator is working?"

"Yep." She nods, only to be interrupted by one of the guards.

"Now that you are returned, our rightful king, you can overthrow him and return our people to glory," one of the still kneeling Roth's says, his face hopeful.

"Bah," Nydo says. He shifts his weight, his strange glowing eyes taking in the prostrate Roth before him.

I squint. There's a restlessness about him though, and I wonder at how long he's beaten himself up over knowing the Roth leader was a total genocidal piece of garbage and living in hiding anyway to protect himself... and his brothers.

"What are you going to do now?" I ask.

"We're going to take these females and the rest of the prisoners and shut down their forward operating base," Michelle answers. "Nydo's identity is now known to the Roth here, so he can't come back to Sueva."

We all stare at the tiny intel analyst.

She blinks back at us owlishly, pushing her glasses back on her nose. "He's too much of a risk to bring to Sueva. If the Roth Overlord knows we're harboring a rival for power, he'll focus on us. It will be an all-out war. We aren't ready for that."

Nydo clenches his fists, and the two Suevans' tails flick behind them. Reif watches the women in the cell, still slumbering peacefully.

"We will not speak of it," the Roth on the floor say, staring at their flaming king with a mixture of awe and terror. "You will save the Roth people. Your secret is safe with us. We will leave this planet and—"

"Silence," Nydo thunders. "Anyone who endangers Sueva or

humanity or even the foul Arco by mentioning my presence will burn. Am I understood?"

Sweat drips down my skin from the heat of his energy manipulation.

"Yes, my king," the Roth chorus as one, pressing their hands to their faces.

Okayyyy. That's a little weird.

"We can't allow you to come back to Sueva," Michelle insists, stubborn as ever. That's Michelle though. Once she's rationalized her way to a logical conclusion, she's not budging.

"My brothers are still Suevan hostages. I will not abandon them again," Nydo says. "I will help your people against the Roth tyrant. Arco will not suffer them either."

Reif bows his head, a sign of respect.

"Besides," Nydo adds, "I scent my mate among the human females. I will not abandon her, either."

Michelle sighs, fixing me with a pained expression.

"You've got to be shitting me," I moan. "Nydo, my man, not *my* king, but *a* king, you can't just sniff a chick and say she's your mate."

"Are you kidding me?" Michelle's lip curls to the side as she huffs a laugh. "Half those romance books you read out loud to us on the ship had the monster sniffing his mate." She affects a deep voice: "MINE!"

Nydo's eyebrows raise, and he looks between us, a skeptical furrow in his forehead. "Human females like this? To be called mine?"

Reif and Alvez look on with interest, Reif tugging at his fin, attempting to feign nonchalance. His avid gaze gives him away.

"Definitely not," Michelle snorts.

"I don't mind it," I counter. "I kind of like it."

Dergoz tucks an arm around me, ignoring the twenty pounds of alien cat around my neck. "Mine," he whispers into my ear. I melt against him, smiling up at his handsome green face.

"Yeah, I guess the lesson here, my alien gentlemen," Michelle pauses, her nose scrunched up in confusion, "Gentlealienmales? Gentlemales? As I was saying, the lesson here is that all human women are different. What might be one lady's catnip is another's poison." She stares pointedly at Alvez, who manages to look slightly contrite, despite his hugely bunching muscles and generally terrifying scarred appearance.

"We should offer the females poison?" Reif asks, utter confusion on his face.

"What is this catnip?" Nydo adds, tilting his head. His flames have mostly banked now, the searing heat replaced by cozy warmth.

"Cheese and crackers, how do you put up with this idiocy?" Michelle throws her hands up in the air, clearly done with all of us.

"We can help you get the females aboard a ship," one of the Roth says, still staring up at Nydo with worshipful eyes.

Ick. I see why Nydo wanted to hide away for a while. It's a *bit* much.

"None of you touch the human females," he hisses. "You've done enough damage." His flames fan high again, and the Roth shrink back.

"Maybe it makes me petty, but I am loving the way you're inspiring your people right now." Nydo glares at me, and I grin at him. "If they're not going to help, then how do you propose we get all these women onto the ships? If I remember correctly, there's a fuck ton of ladder steps between here and the ground floor."

"There is a second exit," the talkative Roth supplies. "Where we have several ships. We can lead you there, my King."

"Yeaaaaaaaah!" Horatio yells.

I rub my ear, wincing. "That's too loud," I reprimand him. "Ears are sensitive."

"Yeaaaaah," Horatio says, much quieter.

Michelle stares at him with round eyes. "You can't tell me that's not freaky."

"It is freaky," Dergoz agrees.

I elbow him in the ribs, only succeeding in hurting myself.

"There are nine human females," Reif says, clearly ready to move us along. "My brother's cell did not open, but he appears in good health. He and I can each carry two, once you release him."

"Right away, oh friend of the King," the Roth says.

"Damn, okay teacher's pet," I mutter, eyebrows raised. "They're really singing a different tune now, huh?"

"I do not hear anyone singing," Dergoz rumbles from behind me.

Michelle sighs, pinching the bridge of her nose. "You can't tell me that's not obnoxious."

"It's endearing."

"Says the woman with a nightmare cat on her shoulders."

"Wanna take this outside, Michelle?"

Michelle snorts, one eyebrow raised. "We both know I'm the better fighter."

"Because you fight dirty."

"My mate fights dirty?" Alvez says, a note of respect and pride in his voice.

"Now is not the time!" Michelle shouts like a drill sergeant. "Let's get these women up and out of here and in a med bay. No Roths allowed around them when they come to. That includes you, Your Highness!" She glares at Nydo like he personally drugged them.

"It's Your Majesty," I correct. "And I'm pretty sure you know that." Frankly, she's right, none of the Roth should be around when these chickadees wake up. They're going to all need some serious therapy.

"We didn't hurt them," another Roth chimes in. "We just took tests to determine if your species is truly compatible with ours."

A surge of heat blasts through the hallway, causing my eyes to water.

"And?" Nydo growls, clearly on edge.

"And they are, my King."

The heat intensifies.

I fan my face. "Can you knock that off, Smokey the Bear?"

Michelle sighs, but the heat ratchets down to something slightly less intense than the surface of the sun. "Smokey the Bear was anti-fire."

"Always a critic," I tell her, but I smile. "Shit yeah. We're free. Alright, crew" —I cup my hands over my mouth— "as nice as this little reunion party has been, let's load up and load out. It's time to get everyone out of here and safe and sound back... on Sueva."

Michelle's eyebrows shoot up in surprise. Like she knows what I was about to say.

Home.

Since when do I think of Sueva as home?

CHAPTER
TWENTY-SIX

BEX

THE BIGGEST ROTH ship has a med bay, and Michelle and I banish the rest of Nydo's newly loyal followers — subjects?— from helping. The clean bright and white room is full of the sound of heavy breathing and the small noises Michelle and I make as we hover over the women, making sure they're okay. Like every med bay ever, it smells of antiseptic and something nameless and metallic that coats my tongue.

No Suevans, no Arco, and definitely no Roth. The last thing we want them to see when they finally wake up is those grey-skinned fuckers. Even if they weren't in charge of this operation, they suck in my eyes.

Suck a big one!

"What?" Michelle asks, scanning one of the limp women with a medical device. We had Tati and Carmen on the comm just a minute ago, and they gave us a short and sweet briefing on how to help the women feel physically and emotionally better when they wake. Well, as much as we can, at least.

"What do you mean, what?" I ask, deciphering the readings on the Roth tech as best I can. Looks fine. Looks like what Tati said to keep an eye out for, everything's normal. They're just… unconscious. Except… I frown, triggering the device again.

"You said, and I quote, suck a big one. You yelled it."

"Oh. Yeah. I meant the Roth who did this can eat a dick."

"You are a delight," Michelle snorts. "You had me worried there for a hot minute."

I grimace at the reading. "Does this look… weird to you?"

"Are you getting high readings on some of the hormones?" She asks, her lips twisted to the side. She's double checking her device, too, and I swallow hard.

"Yup."

"Let's call Tati and Carmen again."

There's no small talk this time. We shuffle to the comm tablet, punching in the information that will connect us to our med crew, and they pick up almost immediately.

"What's wrong?" Carmen asks as a way of greeting. She's the sweetest of the eight of us, but she's all business right now.

"We're getting a strange reading," I start.

"On the women's hormones," Michelle finishes.

"Hmmm," Carmen says, her voice strained. "Bex, you said they knocked you out, too, right? But you feel okay?"

"Yeah, I'm fine."

"Scan her," Carmen commands Michelle in her take-no-shit doctor voice.

"What are you thinking…" My voice trails off as Michelle obediently waves the wand-thingy over me, then crinkles her nose.

"Hers are high too. Let me scan myself, as a control." She does as she says, and I wait, feeling nauseated. "Mine are fine."

Tati and Carmen share a knowing look. Tati bites her lip, and my stomach bottoms out.

"Show me Bex's readout," Carmen says.

Michelle does so, and they both lean forward to read the results from their comm tablet screen.

"Is this the same readout the other women received?" Tati asks brusquely.

"Here." I pass it to her, not wanting to know what mine says. "This is one of the captives."

"The same," Tati lets out a low whistle. "Okay, you want the good news of the bad news?"

"Bad news," I answer immediately. I don't even have to think about it.

"It looks like they injected you with something to make you ovulate. Like… a lot. Super high luteinizing hormone."

My brow furrows in confusion, and Carmen waves her hand. "You might produce multiple eggs in the next few days."

"Eggs? I'm going to lay an egg?" I scream.

"No, don't lose your head," Tati says, and I can tell she's choking back a laugh. "Most post-pubescent women ovulate once a month and produce one egg, more rarely two or three."

"With luteinizing hormone this high…" Carmen looks at Tati, and I can tell they're both doing some swift calculations.

"Eight?"

"A dozen?" Carmen hazards.

"Are you fucking kidding me? A DOZEN?! I'm not made to carry a LITTER of alien-human babies!" I'm shouting at the tablet, rubbing my lower stomach, as if it's the egg laying off-switch.

"Then do *not* have unprotected sex anytime soon," Tati says cheerily. "Easy as pie."

"Isn't it?" Carmen asks archly. "Or do you have something to tell us?"

"Er—"

"GOOD FOR YOU," Tati yells at me, clapping her hands. "So glad it worked out. But yeah. If you get the nookie, you might have a litter of babies. So don't do that. It would be dangerous for you and your hybrid spawn."

"Don't call my litter that!" I admonish.

Michelle sighs and scrubs a hand over her face. "You're not going to have a litter. Just don't have sex."

"Fine," I say gruffly.

"What the hell are y'all talking about?" a new voice asks. "I'm not about to start shooting out puppies, am I? Where the fuck am I, anyway?"

On the screen, Carmen and Tati's eyes both get huge. "Looks like you're going to have your hands full, good luck!" Carmen says cheerily.

The screen goes black.

Michelle and I stare at each other.

"Y'all just gonna look at each other or are you gonna nut up and answer me?" The woman's voice is slightly frantic now, and I take a deep breath and utter a phrase I never thought I'd say in real life.

"You've been abducted by aliens. They were trying to use you for a breeding program. We're rescuing you. Technically, we already have rescued you. Past tense. Yay! You've been rescued." I beam at them, as though a Miss America grin will soften the blow.

"Why are you lookin' at me like that?" The redhead says, a perplexed look on her face. Her curly, fire-engine red hair sticks out every which way, and her confusion turns into a deep scowl as she pats her stomach. "I don't already have a bun in the oven? Or a whole loaf of babies in there? A dozen? A baker's dozen? They didn't—"

I see the moment panic hits her, the realization of *what might have been* pummeling her with all the subtlety of a glitter-dipped sledgehammer.

"No!" I shout at her, and she flinches back. "They didn't. You aren't. There are no buns. No buns, no loaves, nothing. Just a bunch of eggs."

"They fuckin' laid eggs in me?" Her lower lip wobbles.

"Cheese and crackers, Bex, what is wrong with you," Michelle mutters. "No eggs, not like that."

"Like what?!" She wails. "Are we making ice cream with them? Lemon curd? A hollandaise? A meringue? Aioli?"

Michelle and I blink at her.

"I worked as a chef before the Roth invasion," she says. "We made a lot of egg-based desserts." Her voice shakes a bit.

"You're ovulating a lot. That's all. Human eggs. Your eggs," Michelle finally tells her.

"Isn't that an egg-cellent development?" I ask her brightly.

"You should shut up," she tells me. Relief sweeps across her freckled face, and she pushes her unruly hair from her face.

"I'm Bex," I say, unbothered by her directive. Frankly, I *could* have handled that better.

"Michelle. And you are?" Michelle asks.

"I'm Leigh. Are we going back to Earth?"

"Ah…" I hedge.

"No. We can't. We're persona non-grata with the Federation after they sold us off to the Suevans for tech," Michelle answers in a no-nonsense tone.

"Holy shit, that was y'all?" She gapes at us.

"We're going to Sueva?" Another woman sits up, groggy and rubbing her eyes.

"Just so you know, they gave us ovulation meds. Other than that we're fine," Leigh tells the newly awake woman. "They rescued us. Past tense." Leigh shoots me a glare that could wither a freshly bloomed flower.

"Yes, well, I see now that I could have approached that differently," I say icily. "But you had a chance to revise, I was thinking on my feet."

"Maybe you should sit down, then," Leigh tells me, scooching off her sickbed and hustling around the room, shaking the other women awake and giving them the bad news.

"That was awful," Michelle says, rubbing her temples.

The door slides open, and the room goes deathly quiet. That is, right before it erupts into angry screams. Leigh flies past me, her fists raised, murder on her face.

"I'll fucking kill you!"

"You could try," a deep voice says, "but I will not allow you to harm yourself, my mate."

I groan.

Fucking Nydo.

CHAPTER
TWENTY-SEVEN

DERGOZ

I NOTICE Nydo is gone before anyone else seems to. I stand, grateful the Roth have at least surrendered peacefully, much more peacefully than I ever would have imagined.

But where has Nydo wandered off to?

Something tells me he is hunting his mate.

"Trouble?" Reif rumbles, standing. His brother shovels food into his mouth, barely sparing us a glance as he attempts to make up for all the calories he missed in the Roth cells in one fell swoop.

"Nydo," I answer.

"Then yes," says Alvez, joining us.

A furious scream echoes off the metallic walls, and we share a brief look before bursting into a sprint.

It takes us no time at all to reach the medical facility where Michelle and my sweet Bex were determined to keep the women under watch until they woke.

"You cannot hope to best me," Nydo's saying, flames wreathing his head.

Reif rolls his eyes at me, slowing at the open door. "Show off," he mouths.

"Step away from the women, Nydo."

"I will gladly step away from the human females," Nydo says smoothly. "So long as my mate steps with me."

"I'm not your mate, you slimy bastard." She lands a punch on his chest, and the fire dies slightly as he manipulates the energy field around him, clearly trying to keep from wounding her.

That is an improvement. I sigh.

"You cannot take a human female," I try to reason with him, "the human female has to choose you."

"What she wants is immaterial."

"Like fuck it is!" The woman shrieks, incensed. The rest of the women crowd closer, murderous intent written on their faces.

"We are mates, little one. There is no avoiding fate. You will fall into my arms and my bed sooner or later."

Alvez huffs out a breath, and in the next instant, the Suevan we call the Gladiator has the rightful King of Roth in a headlock, so powerful the other alien is unconscious in a matter of moments.

"I'll cut his nuts off," the wild-haired woman says, looking around, presumably, for a sharp instrument.

"As satisfying as it may be to watch you castrate him, little female," Alvez supplies, "we need the King of Roth intact. He might be the key to ending the Roth Overlord's reign, once and for all. Once the Overlord is dead, you can neuter him at your leisure. Or not."

"What's he talking about?" The woman narrows her eyes in suspicion at Bex and Michelle. "My translator doesn't give me anything for Suevan. Just fucking *Roth*." She spits the word like it's poison.

Michelle blows out a breath and translates for Alvez, who looks at her with a lovestruck gaze. She glances up at him warily, only to immediately divert her attention elsewhere.

"The fucking lost king of Roth?" She puts her hand over her face and screams. "My life is a nightmare!"

Several women behind her tilt their heads, then nod them in apparent agreement. "Her life *is* a nightmare," one agrees.

"I don't want to go where he's going," the flame-haired woman says emphatically.

"You could come to Arco instead of Sueva," Reif says, flexing his muscles. Several of the human females eye him appreciatively. "I will not lie to you, we have need of beautiful females as much as the Suevans and Roth do. But we have treasures under our seas, cities the likes of which you have never seen. You will be honored guests among our people, unless you decide, of course, to become one of our people. You will be treated like queens, and beholden to no one but yourselves."

"That does sound pretty good," a yellow haired woman says.

"So those are our options. Sueva or Arco?"

We all nod, and Reif waves his fins a little, holding his chin high.

"Fuck."

"Okay," Bex claps her hands. "That's enough of that. You have plenty of time to decide. At least an hour." The smile on her face wavers a little, then returns, slightly too bright. "We aren't beholden to the Federation anymore, so if you want to stay here with the Roth, that's cool. Otherwise we leave for Sueva—"

"Or Arco," Reif interjects, smiling at the clearly still half-asleep human females.

"Or Arco," Bex agrees, "in an hour. Enough time to eat and shower and get a move on. And no sex in the meantime, unless you want to get pregnant with a litter of alien-human hybrids."

"On account of all the eggs. Ovulation meds," the flame-haired human clarifies.

"Fascinating," Reif says softly. "I had no idea humans had litters of eggs."

"We don't," Michelle snaps at him. "Now take your big muscles out of here and move the gun show elsewhere."

"I did not bring a gun," Reif argues. "I did not know I would need a gun."

"OUT!" Michelle yells.

"Come with me, my Bex," I say. "Let the others feed the women as they decide their fate."

She nods once, and weariness slips over her as she steps to my side.

I treasure it, that she lets her strong façade drop with me. That she allows me a hint of how she really feels, of who she truly is.

All of her is a gift.

Now, I need to speak on the subject of my forgiveness. On why I acted so rashly, so impulsively as to tie her up.

"Come," I say, holding out my hand. She takes mine in hers, her tiny soft fingers so smooth against my scaled palm. I could touch her for days, weeks even, and it would not be enough.

I only hope she lets me.

I lead her into a small chamber, what looks to be sleeping quarters.

"That went well." She crumples to the ground, pulling her knees up to her face.

"Truly?"

"No, it went over as well as cold cat shit on a rug in the middle of the night. Speaking of cat shit, where's Horatio?"

"Eating." Truly, it terrifies me how much the creature eats. It's alarming at best. At the rate he eats, he should double in size in the next week. I know, because Nydo did the calculation with a gleeful look in his eye, the ass.

"Oh, good for him." She picks at her shirt, then stretches her legs out long in front of her.

"Are you hungry?" I ask, pacing in front of her.

"I could eat, but I'll wait until we're spaceside. I don't trust anything here." She purses her lips, studying me carefully. "What's wrong?"

"I feel that I have not earned your forgiveness, despite

bringing you to orgasm many times. I feel I do not... deserve your forgiveness."

Her jaw drops open, and then she quickly shuts it with a snap. Sighing, she runs her hands through her hair, and despite however long we were knocked out by the dishonest Roth, she seems tired.

"I mean, yeah. I'm still unhappy with your choice to tie me up. But..."

I squat next to her, my tail lashing behind me. Hope wells in me.

"But I... like you."

"You like sex with me? I could give you more orgasms now," I offer.

"No!" she shouts, and I startle at her tone. "No," she repeats, shaking her head. "I don't want a baker's dozen of babies running around."

"I am confused about what that means."

"They pumped me full of medicine to make me more fertile. I don't want a baby right now. I might be ready to try a relationship with you, believe it or not, but I'm not ready for a baby. Let alone twelve babies."

"That would be many young. A blessing indeed."

"It would be dangerous for the babies and me. Humans are only meant to carry one at a time. Three or four at most, and even that gets dicey."

I shake my head. "You honor me by simply speaking of children."

Her whole face scrunches up, and I realize she does not feel comfortable speaking of bearing my loin fruit.

"You do not want to carry the fruit of my loins?"

"Oh, I do *not* like that term at all." She laughs. "And that's not what I'm saying. I'm trying to tell you—" She reaches for me, and I sit next to her, taking her hand and staring into her deep brown eyes. "—that I wouldn't want to bring a baby into this world when you and I are still on rocky ground."

I gaze at the floor, then back at her, in confusion.

"Metaphorically. You and I have a lot of work to do as part-ners, in a relationship, before we could even think about having a baby. Seriously."

"You do seem very serious. It is out of character for you."

"I know, right?" She grins then, but it melts from her face too quickly for my liking. I did not realize how much I looked forward to her smile until it was gone.

"See, that's the thing, Dergoz. I'm not good at relationships. I never have been. It's easy to be ridiculous and make a joke and pretend like everything's good and fine, but when it comes down to it, I run. I like sex, I like men… males," she clears her throat, "but I like being on my own, too. It's one thing to be in bed with someone at night and another to wake up beside them in the morning."

I watch her face, studying the way her mouth moves as she works through her thoughts. "I am grateful you are sharing this with me. I swear to you, Ree-becca, that I will make it as easy as I can for you. I have already made it so much harder than it needed to be. I am a stubborn male though, and I cannot promise to be perfect. I will try as hard as I can. For you, I would try anything. Tell me what you need."

She hunches forward, poking at a fresh hole in the knee of her pants. "That's the problem, Dergoz. I don't know what I need, because I never let myself get this far with anyone. I never let myself get invested in anyone… the way I am with you."

I sit down next to her, holding her sweet hand close to my chest, savoring this vulnerable side of her. Falling in love with it, this quiet part of her she holds so close, hiding it under her easy jokes and easier laughter. "Then tell me what other humans do to support their partners. Tell me of the mating rituals."

Bex grins at me, then rests her head on my shoulder. "Mating rituals. Well, you know, I think I mentioned this to you before, but I think I've managed to make it to near thirty years old with getting all my relationship ideas from romance novels. Thus, the whole monster fucker thing. Which, I feel like I should keep apologizing for, too."

My heart tightens in affection for this woman. "It is true," I admit, "that the term burned me. But I have already forgiven you for it. How could you know that it would wound me so? I know now that you did not mean it the way I interpreted it. We have had our fair share of communication problems." I lift her hand, pressing a kiss to her knuckles, and she shifts against me. Her cheek raises where it's pressed against my arm, and I know she's smiling.

It warms my heart to think of it.

"Tell me how I can make you feel comfortable with the idea of being married to me."

"I don't know." Her shoulder shifts as she shrugs. "In the books I love, they always have these huge, fancy dates."

"I will have to read these books you speak so highly of for research." My eyes narrow. It should not be too difficult to remotely hack the Earth libraries. Translating them might be a bigger job, but if these are the texts and manuals my little mate wants me to emulate, then study them, I will.

"You could get our books here?" She sits up, looking me full in the face. "Why didn't I think of that? I would love to have some reading material again."

"Then I will do it as soon as we are back home. On Sueva," I add belatedly. Perhaps my human still does not think of Sueva as home. I have to say, I would not blame her if she did not.

"That would be seriously amazing," she says, a low laugh tickling across my skin as she leans against me once more. "Talk about a grand gesture. I would say it's real Beauty and the Beast shit to give me a library, but I don't think you'd get that reference."

"They call me the Brute," I remind her, perplexed. "The Beast is married to Abby, and he is a thousand times worse than I ever considered being."

She laughs again, and I try to memorize the sound, half-closing my eyes as I bask in her pleasure.

"Any chance you can get Earth movies, too, when you start our Intergalactic Library Loan program?"

"Anything for you," I tell her, kissing her forehead, completely unable to resist pulling her closer. She is the sun, and I am as surely caught in her orbit as any planet. "What else?"

"I mean, that's plenty. That would seriously make me so happy—" Her words cut off suddenly, as though she has just realized something. "You know…"

"Tell me," I implore. Anything for more of her laughter. More of this honest, tranquil side of her, completely at ease with me. The Brute. I will never stop marveling at her acceptance of me, in spite of everything.

Perhaps because of it.

She clears her throat again, the sound nervous. Her finger pokes at the threadbare knee of her pants. "I never… I don't want you to take this the wrong way. But I always imagined if I were to get married, I'd have a big wedding."

"You did have a big wedding." I frown. "You could not get much larger than the gathering we held at Acriset when you arrived."

"Right. I mean a human wedding. With human traditions. A big white dress. All the parties that go along with it."

"You would choose to marry me again?" I say, ridiculously pleased with her.

"On Earth, in America, where I'm from, at least, the man — male— usually proposes to the female. With a ring and down on one knee, and it's usually very romantic." Her voice is wistful. "Then there are parties that lead up to the wedding, and presents for the married couple, and it's… very traditional and silly, I guess. I mean, we're already married, right?"

"If this is what you want, then I will make it happen. I will research these traditions in your beloved textbooks, and I will deliver on your dream, my Ree-becca. You had your dream stolen from you when you were forced here by your Federation. If these are the things that will make you happy, and relaxed, and pleased with me as your husband, then it is nothing for me to do this for you."

She stares at me, her mouth slightly open in surprise at my easy acquiescence.

"I wonder how males of your species truly behave if me wanting to honor your wishes causes such shock."

"Any conclusions you draw are likely correct," she says grudgingly. "Okay. Well. I don't know what else to tell you I want, then. I guess maybe this type of thing. Where we talk to each other. Where we act like true partners. Where you don't leave me tied up to protect me." She narrows her eyes meaningfully.

"I never really thanked you," I realize out loud. "For rescuing me. I thought you were a weak and foolish female and you have proved me wrong at every turn. I could not ask for a better mate."

A wide grin stretches her full lips, and I cannot stop myself. My hand finds the back of her head like it is the only thing that matters in the whole world, and my lips close over hers, sealing my promises to her with a world-shattering kiss.

When we finally pull apart, she's breathless and the delicious aroma of her arousal wraps tight around me.

She studies me for a long moment, her brown eyes darting across my face before she sighs heavily.

"You never told me what you want from me," she finally says.

Quicker than thought, I lift her to my lap, so that I can look upon her at my leisure. Her eyes go heavy, her lust driving me to the brink.

"I want exactly what you have already given me, Ree-becca. Your honesty. Your smiles and laughter. Your strange and too-sweet home baked treats. Your patience and your determination. Your bravery and your beauty."

Her lower lip wobbles, water forming in her eyes. "Oh. Wow. Well that's really sweet of you."

"I have been a fool, not to see the ample treasure right before me," I growl, unable to resist squeezing her full ass.

She lets out a little squeak that turns into a laugh.

A knock sounds at the door, and we both startle.

"The Earth females have made up their minds. It's time to leave," Alvez calls. "I am not opening the door, Brute, so please do not lose your temper. But please do hurry up finishing whatever it is… you two are working on."

Growling, I squeeze her ass again, rocking her over the hard bulge in my pants.

Alvez makes an annoyed sound, followed by footsteps receding.

"We should go," she says, then writhes a little, her eyes rolling back in her head. "Fuck."

"You said we cannot."

"We definitely cannot… but there are other things we can do to have fun." Her eyes grow speculative, then a slow smile lights up her face. "You know, we should have some alone time on the trip back."

I thrust my hips up, and she rewards me with another moan, her heat driving me crazy through the light fabric of our pants.

"We can't," she says, then confounds me with an aggressive kiss that nearly has me flipping her on her back.

"We could," I say, but I lift her off of me, watching her lust-addled gaze sweep over me.

"Okay," she says, patting her hair. "Okay. I'm fine. Just some hormonal overload." She wags a finger at me. "No sex."

"I am yours to command," I tell her.

"Ugh, I said no sex." She rolls her eyes.

I stare at her in confusion.

"Come on," she says, tugging at my hand.

"Do you think you can lift me from the floor?"

"Absolutely not, but objects in motion and all that," Bex says, huffing slightly as she yanks on my arm.

"I am coming," I tell her. "Not the way I would prefer to be, but I am coming."

"Oh," she crows in delight, her beautiful eyes wide. "You made a sex joke! Good for you!"

I smile at her, and the door hisses open as I tap the control panel.

It's time to find out what fate the human females have chosen.

BEX

SPACE BLURS AROUND US, stars streaking across the viewscreens like miniature comets, like fireflies caught on low shutter speed. It's incredible, no matter how many times I see it.

Half the women are coming back to Sueva with us, the other half up for an adventure on Arco with Reif and his brothers. Apparently their promise of treating the women like queens was appealing enough to outweigh the whole living underwater thing.

I shudder. I've never had mermaid dreams, but good for them. The thought of all that blue water overhead, all around me, never knowing what's lurking in the dark depths…

Ick.

I wrinkle my nose. Though, maybe, space isn't all that different.

Then again, I'm not going to live in space. Inasmuch as a planet isn't living in space, I guess.

"You seem deep in thought," Dergoz says calmly, rubbing my forearm gently.

He can't seem to stop touching me. Normally, I wouldn't like it. I think it would make me feel too trapped, like he was too needy.

Maybe it's the stupid fertility drugs the Roth shot me full of, but right now? I love it. I crave it.

"Just thinking about space," I tell him.

He follows my gaze to the viewscreens, watching the stars whizz by. "It never manages to disappoint me. It should be... claustrophobic, perhaps, the feeling of the vast emptiness closing in. I used to despise it. But somehow, now, I like it. It seems instead," he pauses, searching for the words. "It seems full of hope, of promise. That life, because of all the darkness, flourishes. The darkness, instead of leeching away life, is the reason for it."

I blink at him. "Wow. That's really... that's really something." Huh. I didn't know he had it in him. "They should have called you the Poet, not the Brute."

"Do poets in your world regularly make their enemies eat their own intestines?"

"Ehhhh... No. I can unequivocally say no. Though we do have a saying about putting your foot in your mouth when you say something stupid."

"And then you force your enemies to eat their feet."

I shake my head, my shoulders stiff with held-in laughter. "Absolutely not. Not literally."

"It does not bother you that I've done this?"

"I mean, do I want to hear about it in gory detail? No. But if you need me to listen, if you need to talk through it, I will. If you need to come to terms with the violence you had to commit to keep your people safe by talking it out, or whatever." I shrug, slightly uncomfortable.

"I am fine with it. I would have done it again if the Roth had hurt you. And that is why they call me the Brute," Dergoz continues.

"That's really romantic," I tell him, fluttering my eyelashes.

"You think me force-feeding people their limbs is romantic?"

"I've read too many orc romances, probably." I snort.

"I must look into these orc creatures you speak of," he says. His tail swishes against the floor, then the heavy weight of it settles against my ankles possessively.

"I mean, feel free, but maybe you should start out with something a little more tame."

"No. If these are the texts you love on the art of human romance, then these are the texts I will study."

I bite my cheeks, my eyebrows rocketing up. "Suit yourself."

"I will. But for now, I want to take you back to my sleeping quarters and lick your cunt until you quiver around me."

"Oh," I say faintly. "Well. Who would I be to say no to that offer?"

His tail strokes against my leg, and wet warmth pools inside my underwear.

"I have thought of another way I can bring you pleasure without the fear of impregnating you," he says, his voice thick with arousal.

It's turning me on, the way he's staring at me like I'm a tasty fookie he's ready to devour. "Oh?" I repeat.

His tail strokes higher on my leg, and I swallow hard. "Are you sufficiently enticed to join me?"

"Yep," I tell him, and before he can do more than smile smugly at me, I turn on my heel, racing toward the sleeping quarters. Most of the women are still sleeping off the effects of stress and capture, but Nydo and the redhead Leigh scowl at each other from across the hall as my feet pound against the ship's floor.

Alvez and Michelle are deep in conversation at a table in the rec room, their heads tilted together over a projected document. Horatio is curled up next to Michelle, who strokes his head absent-mindedly as she talks. They're cute, and I have a feeling it won't be long until Michelle finally gives in and gets some, too.

Footsteps echo behind me, and I squeal in anticipation. I've always wanted to be chased by a big alien hottie, then thoroughly dicked down. Living the dream over here. I get to the door just as huge hands wrap around me, and I yelp again, then dissolve into laughter as Dergoz gently tickles my ribs. The door slides open, and Dergoz swoops me into his arms, kissing me thoroughly. Aggressively.

Perfectly.

The door closes behind us, and he snarls a little, his fang showing as he tosses me onto the bed, where I bounce slightly in the artificial gravity.

Then he's on me, pinning me to the soft mattress as his mouth closes over mine. Stealing my breath, stealing my thoughts. I wrap my legs around him, or try to, but fail miserably, considering our ridiculous size difference… that I love.

"You think you can outrun me?" he asks.

"Remind me to show you this vampire movie whenever you successfully hack Earth digital media," I manage, laughing.

"Is this another monster romance?"

"I guess it is," I agree, winding my arms around his neck and fastening onto him like a horny barnacle. His hair falls in thick strands down his back, and I run my fingers through it as he gazes down at me, affection clear in every line of his face.

"May I tell you what I would like to do to you now?" He traces a claw over my cheekbone, and I shudder, wet and ready already.

"I would like that very much," I tell him.

"I cleaned my tail for you," he says succinctly.

"Oh? Oh! *Ooooh.*" I blink. "You want to…"

"I want to bring you close to orgasm with my mouth, then thrust my tail into you until you come all around it."

"I am down to clown," I say hurriedly, shucking my pants and shirt faster than warp speed.

"You are down… to clown?"

"Yes, yes, I mean yes," I say, pushing my nakedness at him and smashing another kiss onto his face. "I am so horny. I can't get enou—"

My words melt into a low, animalistic sound as his mouth

closes around my clit, his fangs pressing on either side, baring my most sensitive part to him.

"So fucking perfect," he snarls, suckling.

I squirm against him, already close to orgasm. Something about that bumpy tongue, the tusks—

I cry out again as his tail strokes against my opening. "Oh, oh," I say, my eyes wide.

"You can take it. You will," Dergoz growls, then sucks my clit again. "You are already wetter than ever, because your whole body wants me inside it. Doesn't it?"

"Yes," I moan. "I want it." Everything clenches in anticipation.

And then his tail strokes again, before fucking me in earnest.

I hold on to his shoulders for dear life, the sensations overwhelming and somehow just right all at once. My orgasm hits almost instantly, the reality of being fucked senseless by my own scales-and-tails warlord even better than the fantasy.

"You will come again," Dergoz commands, and this time, he slides a blunted finger around my ass.

"Feels... so," I pant, unable to even get a full sentence out. Unable to do anything but come again, the fullness of his tail and finger and tongue driving me over the edge faster than I ever thought possible.

I'm slick with sweat, slick with my own arousal, and Dergoz keeps going, watching me as I ratchet towards another orgasm. This might be what kills me. Death by multiple orgasms.

What a way to go.

"Too much," I tell him. My legs are shaking, my arms quivering.

"Take it," he snarls, and I do. Oh my God, I do.

This time, when I recover enough to look up at him, he pulls away, absolutely satisfied, smirking down at me. His cock is hard against his pants, and suddenly, I want nothing more than to wipe that smirk off his face and give him a taste of his own medicine.

"My turn," I say huskily. His pants come undone easily, his huge cock swinging free, bobbing in front of my face.

When I take him in my mouth, I manage to become aroused all over again. Got to be the fertility drugs. Or maybe it's just… Dergoz. Maybe it's the fact I have this brutal alien warlord at my mercy, perfectly devoted to me. Loving me.

Wanting me despite all of my many flaws.

I slide my tongue over him, enjoying his salty taste, enjoying his murmured sounds of pleasure. His xof begins vibrating against my nose, and I laugh a little, taking him deeper, until I have to inhale carefully to avoid gagging on his huge cock.

Carefully, I touch the vibrating xof, and he groans, the sound nearly one of pain, before he tangles his hand in my hair.

I keep waiting for him to push himself further into my mouth, the thought of being used thoroughly by this male turning me on all over again. Impossibly so.

But he doesn't. He simply waits.

It's really sweet how gentle he is with me. How concerned he is with my pleasure, with my enjoyment of even giving him this blow job.

And enjoy it I do—I love the little noises he makes as I work his cock with my mouth, sucking and nibbling. The way he looks at me like I'm driving him out of his mind.

When he finally groans, I swallow his cum down, then lean back on my elbows.

It's my turn to be smug, and smug I am indeed.

I bagged an alien warlord, and even though it took a while to get here, I couldn't be happier with how it's working out.

CHAPTER
TWENTY-NINE

DERGOZ

THE NIGHT AIR is chill despite the atmospheric bubble over Edrobaz. Males eat awkwardly, all of us unsure what exactly to do during this so-called bachelor party my Ree-becca insisted upon.

Nydo's brothers have joined us in Edrobaz, as a term of his aiding with the rescue on Nyria. It is strange to see the grey skin of our former enemies mingled among the green of Sueva, but I cannot deny that the three of them have shown me a new side of the Roth.

Though Nydo will likely never be my favorite person.

Draz, in particular, stares at him with open loathing, no doubt still dwelling on what he did to him and his mate those weeks ago.

But even Draz cannot deny that the lost Roth King has proven useful.

So we all stand, drinking the fizzy bitter drinks our people prefer to celebrate with. Festive banners drape between the myza, and we all keep trying not to look at a strange loaf my mate baked in the shape of what appears to be female breasts.

"So," Alvez begins. "What have you been doing in your spare time lately?"

The Beast begins to laugh, but the sound cuts off quickly as he snarls, pacing in front of the breast-loaf. "She does this to aggravate me," he says to no one in particular.

"Reading human romance texts," I tell him. "They are full of information on how to woo a female. Human courtship is very strange."

Every male steps closer, determination and intent clear on their faces.

"Tell us what you have learned," Nydo commands. "How do you please a human female?"

"Strangely, in many of the books I have studied, they love to be kidnapped. It appears to be something of a custom for their people."

The Suevan Warlords all raise their eyebrows. Kanuz, the prince, lets out a low laugh. "I do not think that is correct," he manages between chuckles.

"Let Dergoz speak," Alvez says thoughtfully. "You were alone with your female for weeks. Perhaps this is what it takes."

"There is a creature called an Orc in many of these romance manuals. The Orc kidnaps the human female, and then feeds her a diet of his cum, which is nutritious."

Kanuz chokes on his drink, and Draz slaps him on the back as they share a look. "I do not think these are accurate texts," Draz advises.

"Perhaps not. But they are my mate's favorites."

"They want to be kidnapped?" Alvez asks, his eyes wide.

"I think it is mostly a fantasy. Of being cared for by a male, of being coveted. I am not sure even my Bex would like this." And she definitely likes drinking my cum. "Perhaps I should try it tonight, though."

"It sounds like an interesting experiment," Alvez says.

"You cannot kidnap your wives," Draz commands.

"Oh, I think you should let them find this out the hard way," Kanuz says. Draz glares at him.

"I like the sound of the hard way," Nydo says.

"Eat the breast loaf," I growl at him, gesturing to the strange thing my wife called a cake. "Fill your mouth with something other than nonsense. I am going to go kidnap my wife. I read one text where the woman's lover stole her away at just such a party as the one the women are having tonight. Perhaps she wants me to do this."

"You plan to take her from her own party?" Nydo asks. "I thought the whole point of this strange human ritual was for the mates to be separated."

"The point of this ritual is that she asked for it," I yell at him. The Roth tries my nerves. It is no wonder that the flame-haired woman, Leigh, avoids him at all costs. He is insufferable. His brothers are less obnoxious, but they hardly ever stand up to him.

"But you think she secretly wants to be stolen away from the human ritual she specifically asked you to honor?" Alvez asks slowly.

Kanuz laughs harder.

"These human females make no sense," the Beast snarls, scooping a handful of breast loaf from the table and into his mouth. "She is driving me insane with her games. Perhaps kidnapping is the only way to make her see the light."

"Abby will gut you if you try," Draz tells him drily.

"He is right," Alvez agrees. "Warlord Abby will pull your eye out and laugh when you stumble around blindly."

"Abby will cut your xof off and shove it up your—"

The Beast cuts Kanuz off with a manic growl. "Fine."

"She is not as accommodating or gentle as some of the human females." Alvez paces, and I raise an eyebrow at Draz.

"I do not think whatever you are thinking is a good idea, Alvez," Draz cautions.

"I am only enjoying my drink." He scowls into his cup.

"Mmm," Draz says noncommittally.

A huge white jono flower blooms in the night air, releasing a spicy floral scent. Luminescent green winged insects flock to it, and I watch them for a moment, collecting my thoughts.

"Are you not enjoying your bachelor party?" Kanuz asks. "Gen thought this was a fun idea, too."

"Are you enjoying it?" I ask him warily.

"I would rather be feeding Steve a haunch of fresh meat," Kanuz answers.

I laugh, knowing how much Kanuz detests feeding the great Crigomar beast that's attached itself to his wife, thanks to her ingestion of a bioluminescent lure. She glows like an actual star, a fact my Ree-becca finds highly amusing.

"I think I will kidnap her," I say. "She asked me to study her romance books. Perhaps she meant for me to come to this conclusion on my own."

Without another word, I turn away from the gathering. I would much rather be with my mate than with the men who only want to interrogate me about the mating habits of humans. I do not like being apart from her.

I make it to my myza quickly, gathering up some silken cords Ree-becca purchased at the market, though she has not made mention of what she planned to do with them. If she did not want me to use them, I imagine she would have told me to leave them alone.

But when I asked her what they were for, she only gave me a strange look and laughed.

My funny little human mate.

The myza door closes quietly behind me, and I move carefully and quietly through the streets of Edrobaz, towards where the human females are having a party of their own. The sound of their laughter colors the night in bright melody. They seem like they must be having more fun than we were at our bachelor party.

Perhaps I was wrong to assume my Ree-becca would like to be kidnapped.

I find that I do not care. I want to see the look of surprise on her face, I want to tie her up in the soft rope like I read in her human romance manual, and I want to show her exactly what she has to look forward to during our life together.

Over and over again.

CHAPTER
THIRTY

I TOSS BACK another one of the sweet, super-fizzy drinks and smile to myself. The women we've brought back from the Roth base are finally starting to loosen up a little, though I think they're going to need a lot more time to really feel safe. Carmen and Tati have been trying to counsel them and provide therapy, and I've been working nonstop with the Suevan techs on getting them improved translator implants.

So far, it's not going great, though.

But tonight is not about that. Tonight is not about all the fucked-up ways we managed to get to Sueva.

Tonight, we are doing something normal. We are celebrating my wedding to my Brute, my Dergoz.

I sigh wistfully, my body going hot and loose all over at the mere thought of him.

"I am so fucking glad you managed to get us something to watch," Gen says through a mouthful of food. "This is literally amazing, and I hate this stupid show."

"Feels like home," Abby says, her feet tucked under her as the blue glow of a vidscreen lights up her face. On the screen, a super old episode of Bachelor in Paradise plays, and the women all groan as one of the bachelors says something completely dramatic. And stupid.

"Suevans aren't the only himbos in the galaxy!" Abby yells, throwing a handful of crackers at the image.

"This isn't the most bitching bachelorette party I've been to, but I have to say, it's probably just right, considering," Gen pats her stomach, which has the cutest little bump now. She's hungry all the time, and I pass her another plate of the herbed crackers she can't get enough of. I make them in bulk for her.

"This was a really good idea," Niki tells me softly, munching on a slice of fruit. "You've really done so much to help everyone feel at home here. More than me or Gen. Getting the books and some entertainment from Earth has really done wonders for them."

"You're busy doing warlord shit, Niki, don't beat yourself up. Besides, I don't mind. It's been super fun getting to help Dergoz with that little side project."

"Well, between that and your cooking up new recipes that remind everyone of home, you've been a real asset. I hope you're proud of yourself."

My eyes tear up a little. It's not that Niki's such a hardass she never praises anyone, but she does reserve her compliments for when she truly means them.

"Are you enjoying your bachelorette party?" she asks.

"Eh," I say. "To be honest… I'd rather be home with Dergoz, curled up with a book."

"That's not all she'd rather be curled up with," Gen says loudly.

"You're not wrong, and if you're trying to embarrass me, you literally can't. I have no shame," I tell her.

Everyone's attention is fixed on the two of us now.

"Then tell us what it's like," Abby finally says. Juls shoots her a look, and even Leigh and some of the new women sit up with interest.

I sigh, a dreamy expression floating across my face.

"They have a vibrating… thing. A xof. And it hits you right where it counts." I bite into a slice of fruit, raising one eyebrow.

"Does it hurt?" Michelle says, her eyes narrowed. "It sounds too intense."

"Oh, it's intense in all the right ways. And his tail… he sure knows how to use it."

"His tail?" Leigh says, her voice ratcheting up to a register only dogs can hear.

"You don't have to worry about that," Abby tells her, "you got grey skin and flames."

Leigh puts a pillow over her face and slumps over.

Juls laughs, but Tati and Carmen are both shaking their heads at Abby.

"It's awesome sex. And the best part is, he listens," I interrupt loudly. "He just wants to please me. In fact, he's been reading romance novels, because he wants to learn what human women like." I can't keep the smile off my face. It's just so darn cute—

The door swings open, and several women squeal in surprise. Abby stands, her hand immediately on her plas pistol. Niki and Gen each stand too, ready to fight. Juls circles the wall, headed to the door to outflank the intruder.

Until we see who it is.

"Who hired the stripper?" Abby asks, relaxing back on the couch.

On the vidscreen, a woman in a gown is bawling as she tears red petals from a rose.

"Dergoz?" I ask, surprised. "Did something happen? Is everything all right?"

"You are coming with me," he says. "You are my mate, and I am kidnapping you, just like they do in the books you like. My semen is not nutritious, but I will still feed it to you."

Tati spits out her drink, soaking Carmen, who stands there dripping in shock.

"Uh," I manage. "Can't say I expected this tonight."

Dergoz advances on me, his tail lashing back and forth furiously as he produces a length of silken cord.

"Oh!" I say, my mouth hanging open in surprise. "You figured out what that was for, huh?"

"No questions, my little human. You are coming with me."

"Alright," I shrug, sliding off the stool and standing on my tiptoes to press a kiss to his face.

Consternated, he stares down at me. "You are supposed to fight me and let me carry you off as you cry."

"This is better than the most dramatic rose ceremony ever," Abby says, cramming food in her mouth.

Gen nods, eyes glued to us.

"You kinky bastard," I tell him breathlessly. "All right, I'll play." I fling the back of my hand and wail. "Noooo, please, don't kidnap me, I'm uh, at my bachelorette party!"

"Wait," Dergoz whispers. "Are you really saying no?"

"No," I tell him, cracking one eye open. "Go ahead and tie me up. I'm playing along."

"They're not going to win any Oscars," Juls says. Leigh snorts, but most of the new women are wide-eyed, though several seem to laugh as they glance at each other.

"I will take you to my bed and ravage you, my mate," Dergoz says roughly, tying my hands behind me.

"Ohhh noooo," I say, winking at Niki, who's shaking her head, her eyes wide in disbelief. "Not that!"

"Yes, that," Dergoz says.

I swallow a laugh, then squeal as he throws me over one shoulder, the cords loose enough to allow me to wave a goodbye.

"And it appears the alien warlord has chosen who to give his rose to after all," Abby deadpans.

Gen high-fives her, and then everyone's waving goodbye as Dergoz sets off at a jog.

When we pass Alvez, who strides by us with a determined look on his face and a bag slung over his shoulder, I think nothing of it.

I'm too busy thinking about all the fun I'm going to have with my Brute.

EPILOGUE

BEX

DERGOZ'S myza is full of mouth-watering scents. I'm exhausted from last night, sore in all the right places, and utterly happy. We're still working on trusting each other, but it turns out relationships are work. Who knew?

I think probably everyone knew.

But it's going really, really well, and right now, I'm sifting through drawings the market vendor has made of potential white wedding gowns as Dergoz cooks my favorite meal for breakfast.

I'm so content in my own little world of domestic bliss I don't even register the knock outside until Dergoz raises an eyebrow at me.

"Are you expecting company, my Ree-becca?"

"No…" I say, drawing out the sound. Gingerly, I get up, wincing slightly.

"I was too hard with you last night," Dergoz growls, guilt flitting over his face.

"No, I'm pretty sure I was too hard with *you* last night," I tell him, laughing.

"Yeaaaaah!" Horatio comments sleepily, then curls back up in his favorite spot in the sunny window.

The knock comes again, causing Horatio to flick his tails back-and-forth in irritation.

Carefully, I make my way to the door, then swing it open wide, coming face-to-face with Niki and Gen. They're wearing their patented you're-in-deep-shit expressions, and I try not to flinch back reflexively.

"What happened?" I ask. "Did the Roth invade Earth? Are they on their way here?"

"No," Niki says, but from her no-nonsense tone, I know something bad's gone down.

"It's those two complete shit-for-brains, Alvez and the Beast," Gen says.

"Do you want breakfast?" Dergoz asks.

"Aww, babe, that's so sweet of you," I tell him. "He can make more for you. He's a great cook."

"No," Niki says.

"Yes," Gen says at the same time. "This baby is hungry."

Niki sighs, scrubbing a hand down her face in sheer annoyance. I stifle a laugh. "We have solman berries."

"Fine," she snaps.

"I will make more, and you will tell us what the warlords did," Dergoz says. There's a flicker of unease in his eyes, and I squint at him until he looks away.

"Abby and Michelle are gone. Vanished in the night."

"What?!" I screech, horrified. "Was there blood? Are they hurt? Did the killer leave a note?"

"Seriously, Bex, sometimes I wonder about you," Gen says, grunting as she settles herself on a stool. "There was no blood." Niki and I join her at the large wooden table next to the Suevan kitchen, and Dergoz flits around, poking at the food.

"No note." Niki narrows her eyes at me. "Did you see anything suspicious when you were leaving the myza last night?"

"No... wait, yes."

Dergoz deposits a steaming plate in front of me, and I give him a quick peck on the cheek. "Thanks, boo."

Gen clears her throat, her expression pained as she stares longingly at my food. "Care to tell us what it was you saw?"

"Alvez. I didn't think anything of it, but he was carrying a bag on his shoulder."

"I fucking knew it," Niki snaps. "Draz said you told everyone at your bachelorette party last night that human females love to be kidnapped."

"I…" Dergoz puts a plate in front of Gen, his tail whipping back and forth in frenzy. Mmm. That tail. My cheeks heat.

"Focus," Gen says, snapping her fingers in front of my face. Then she shovels some food into her mouth, and her eyes go distant. "Yum."

"You two are driving me insane. Dergoz, did you tell the men to kidnap their women?"

"I may have said that the romance manuals Bex recommended featured kidnapping as a mode of courtship."

"Fuck," Niki says, then places her forehead on the table. "So Alvez definitely took Michelle. You didn't see the Beast?"

"No one would see the Beast if he doesn't want to be seen," Dergoz says easily.

"What does that mean?" Niki asks, her nose scrunched up.

"He can camouflage himself. Turn near invisible, especially at night. It is a very handy genetic mutation."

"Great. The Beast is also the invisible man. That's just fucking great."

"We all told him she would take his balls and wear them as a necklace if he tried to take her. We all know Warlord Abby is fearsome and mean in a fight."

"I tell you she's been kidnapped by an invisible alien and your first response is that you warned him she'd maim him? And he did it anyway?" Gen's voice goes up an octave. "Ridiculous." She bursts into tears.

Ugly tears, too, not cute ones. Her face turns blotchy and red, her nose running.

Dergoz's eyes are huge in alarm, his tail slashing behind him.

"Uh, Gen," I say. "Are you okay?"

"It's called HORMONES, OKAY?! WHY IS EVERYONE SO MEAN TO ME?!" Gen keeps eating, sobbing into her food.

Niki averts her eyes, then pinches the bridge of her nose. "Carmen said that her progesterone levels are much higher than normal, probably because of the hybrid baby."

"Right," I say calmly, handing Gen a soft cloth to wipe her nose on. "Okay, then. Are the other women safe?"

"They're furious. Especially the new ones."

"They have had SUCH A HARD TIME," Gen wails.

"So what do we do?" I ask. "Want to send a search party out?"

Dergoz laughs, a low sound.

We all turn to him. Gen raises a finger, murder in her eyes. She glows slightly brighter in her fury. "You don't get to LAUGH!"

Dergoz's mouth snaps shut.

"Explain, Dergoz."

"You cannot find them. The Beast is an expert at subterfuge. Alvez, The Gladiator, is not as good as the Beast, but he will not allow himself to be easily tracked. Have you tried their comms?"

"Not yet," Niki says grudgingly.

"Try their comms. Make sure the women are safe, and worst case, we can ask you and your husband to make a royal decree to bring the human females home immediately."

Gen stops crying, clearly mulling it over. "I should have thought of that."

She pushes her chair back, and Niki stands too, obviously still annoyed. Horatio checks them out with one eye before deciding to go back to napping. I scratch his head as the two women say goodbye, clearly intent on solving this problem ASAP.

I've never been more relieved I didn't join the warlord trials.

Leadership? No, thanks.

As soon as the door closes, I round on Dergoz. "You already had that plan ready to go, didn't you?"

"I must admit, I was slightly troubled by seeing Alvez last night." He slowly blinks at me. "Are you angry with me?"

"No," I say. "It's not your fault they made a bad choice. It wasn't great you put that idea in their head… but who knows? Maybe it will turn out for the best."

For Michelle and Alvez, I'm nearly positive it will. Those two have been dancing around each other for weeks now.

The Beast and Abby? I have some doubts.

But when Dergoz wraps his hands around my waist, tugging me close, all my worries flee.

There's just him and me, and right now, that's enough.

He's all I need.

Horatio screams at me, and I reach down, scratching him behind the ears.

Horatio is pretty great, too.

———

If you enjoyed reading this book, please consider leaving a review. Reviews help indie authors be seen by new readers, which means I get to keep writing!

To never miss a release, sign-up for my newsletter here.

Next up is Michelle and Alvez's book, Wed To The Alien Gladiator.

And stay tuned for more about Nydo, the lost king of Roth…

ALSO BY JANUARY BELL

ACCIDENTAL ALIEN BRIDES

Wed To The Alien Warlord

Wed To The Alien Prince

Wed To The Alien Brute

Wed To The Alien Gladiator

Wed To The Alien Beast

Wed To The Alien Assassin

Wed To The Alien Hunter

Wed To The Alien Rogue

ALIEN DATING GAMES

Alien Tides

BOUND BY FIRE

Alien On Fire

FATED BY STARLIGHT

Following Fate: Prequel Novella

Claimed By The Lion: Book One

Stolen By The Scorpio: Book Two

Taurus Untamed: Book Three

ABOUT THE AUTHOR

January Bell writes steamy fantasy and sci-fi romance with a guaranteed happily ever after. Combining pure escapism, a little adventure, and a whole lotta love makes for romance that's a world apart. January spends her days writing, herding kids and ducks, and spends the nights staring at the stars.

For the latest updates, follow me on Instagram and TikTok.

www.ingramcontent.com/pod-product-compliance
Lightning Source LLC
Chambersburg PA
CBHW061349310726
48974CB00001B/258